WHEN I MET YOU

A Christian Romance

JULIETTE DUNCAN

Water's Edge Series- Book 1

Cover Design by http://www.StunningBookCovers.com

Copyright © 2021 Juliette Duncan

All rights reserved.

WHEN I MET YOU is a work of fiction. Names, characters, and incidents are all products of the author's imagination or are used for fictional purposes. Any mentioned brand names, places, and trade marks remain the property of their respective owners, bear no association with the author, and are used for fictional purposes only.

THE HOLY BIBLE, NEW INTERNATIONAL VERSION®, NIV® Copyright © 1973, 1978, 1984, 2011 by Biblica, Inc.™ Used by permission. All rights reserved worldwide.

Praise for "When I Met You"

"Juliette Duncan did it again! What a wonderful story of how God can use anybody no matter what their life has been like in the past. " - *Mae*

"If you like clean, inspiration, heartfelt stories, you can't go wrong with 'When I Met You'. I highly recommend."- *SJ*

"I loved reading Lucas and Amelia's story. It reminded me that once we have been forgiven for things we did in the past we need to forget those mistakes and move forward into what God has planned for our lives. The 'pop-up' prayers made the book even more real as that's exactly what we do in real life when we are in trouble or even thankful for something - pop a prayer! Grab a copy of this book and read it, you won't be dissapointed." - *Anne*

"This is a beautiful story! Such an inspirational book telling of God's grace and mercy. A sweet romance intertwined in the story of Lucas and Amelia. All of the characters are wonderful and each plays a part in the lives of the young couple. Christian love and service are an integral part of the plot and show how important it is for Christians to reach out to the people around them. I felt encouraged by this story when I finished." -*Faith*

Forward

HELLO! Thank you for choosing to read this book - I hope you enjoy it! Please note that this story is set in Australia. Australian spelling and terminology have been used and are not typos!

As a thank you for reading this book, I'd like to offer you a FREE GIFT. That's right - my FREE novella, "Hank and Sarah - A Love Story" is available exclusively to my newsletter subscribers. Go to: http://www.julietteduncan.com/subscribe to claim your copy now and to be notified of my future book releases. I hope you enjoy both books! Have a wonderful day!

Juliette

FORWARD

Prologue

Amelia Anderson fled from Water's Edge Bar and Tavern and tripped on the concrete steps, barely catching herself as hot tears stung her eyes. Gasping, she pressed her hands to her face, sharp breaths hissing past her lips.

How dare he!

She'd worked in places like this her entire life. As a bartender, she was used to inappropriate remarks and unsolicited invitations from the men who hung around the counter. But, ugh, that leering middle-aged man...

She was sick of men like him treating her however they wished.

There had to be more to life.

But what?

Hands trembling, she pulled a cigarette and lighter from her apron pocket. In past years, she wouldn't have thought twice about a customer's lustful words. It came with the territory. But tonight, when she'd refused to let that man's degrading speech slide over her, her boss had called her inhospitable and said that, if she couldn't do her job, she could take a hike.

Take a hike? Although new, she was the best and most experienced barmaid he had.

She wasn't soft, but that creep should have been thrown out. Not her.

She lit the cigarette and took a long, slow drag. And then another.

She closed her eyes and slunk against the brick wall. Three more hours. How could she go back into that cesspit? Her stomach roiled, but she needed the job.

Her head snapped up at the lilt of piano music from the church across the road. Weird having a church opposite this sleazy bar. She opened her eyes. A man carrying a book under one arm propped open the front door before disappearing into the brightly lit sanctuary.

She finished her cigarette as churchgoers pulled into the car park and made their way inside. She was about to light up another when a short middle-aged woman climbed out of a station wagon. As she closed the door, her gaze landed on Amelia.

Amelia sunk further into the wall and averted her gaze. Since arriving in town a week earlier, she'd laid low. She'd bought groceries at the corner store at odd hours and gone back and forth from the apartment she shared with two other bartenders. That was it. She didn't want to get to know anyone. Water's Edge was a pit stop, just as her last town had been. And the town before.

The soft patter of white tennis shoes stopped in front of her. Sighing, she raised her head.

The woman stood before her, a cheerful smile bunching up her round face. Strands of silvery hair, twisted into a bun at her nape, escaped to tangle in the equally silvery necklace laying over her ruffled blouse. A cross glinted from it.

Amelia groaned. That's all she needed. A Goody Two-shoes.

The woman's smile broadened. "Hello."

Angling her head, Amelia stood with folded arms while the woman rabbited on.

"I'm Charlotte Brown. I own the diner here in Water's Edge. You must be new in town." She waved a pudgy little hand, polish-free nails, only one ring. "I know just about everyone. No one passes up the diner's weekend lunch specials. What's your name, dear?"

Dear? Seriously? No one had called her 'dear' in a long time. If ever.

"Amelia." Her eyes narrowed, and her lips pursed.

The corners of the woman's brown eyes crinkled as she extended her hand. "Nice to meet you."

Really? How could this respectable woman think it was nice to meet *her*?

Although her hand smelled of beer and the skulls on her rings would no doubt offend this gentle lady, Amelia accepted the gesture and took her hand. That soft hand—or maybe it was the woman's whole persona—wrapped around her like a cuddly blanket and drew her in.

Peering at Amelia, the woman lowered her brow. "Are you all right?" Her voice was as soft and embracing as her hand. "You look like you've had a rough night."

Amelia blinked back tears. Rough night? What an understatement. "Yeah, but it comes with the job."

"You work in the bar?"

Here it came—the condemnation. Shedding the woman's hand, Amelia ground her teeth and tightened her arms over her chest. "Yep."

The woman nodded to the church. "Service is about to begin. Would you care to join me?"

Join her? Amelia frowned. She hadn't set foot in a church in years. Her parents had never been much for getting right with God on Sundays. But this woman's kindness and the strong urge to turn her back on the bar had her thinking.

It could be just the thing. Wasn't she looking for something?

The woman patted Amelia's forearm. "We can slip in the back. We won't disturb anyone."

The assurance that she, a black sheep, wouldn't be paraded down the aisle in front of the citizens she'd so diligently avoided sealed the deal. She took a deep breath. "Okay. Why not?"

The woman's smile threatened to stretch off her face. "Excellent! Come along, then."

Amelia had nothing to lose by playing hooky to attend church, except her job. But she'd planned to move on soon anyway, so what did it matter? She followed the woman—*Charlotte?*—across the road.

Who'd have guessed that not only would she lose her job but also her impromptu church trip would change her life?

Chapter One

Two days had passed since Charlotte invited her to church. Amelia's experience at the Water's Edge Community Church and Pastor Noah's words about God's love had touched her so deeply that, by the end of the service, she'd given her heart to the Lord.

The peace and reassurance Charlotte and the other churchgoers possessed was unlike anything Amelia had ever experienced, and she wanted to be part of it. And so, less than an hour after Amelia fled those creeps, Charlotte led her through a simple prayer asking Jesus to forgive her of her sins and save her by His amazing grace. Charlotte explained that, accepting Christ into her heart wasn't the end of her journey, it was the beginning. She'd need to seek the Lord every day to strengthen her relationship with Him and grow in her faith.

With no idea how it would all look or even fully understanding it all, Amelia had been ready to do just that. It had to be better than serving leering creeps at dodgy bars.

And now, here she was, about to meet a prospective new roommate. If only she could light up a cigarette. She'd lived in so many places and roomed with countless girls over the years, but meeting Willow Kelley felt different. Charlotte had assured her Willow was a lovely girl and they'd get on just fine. But *she* wasn't a lovely girl, and *she* wasn't sure they would. How could Charlotte be so sure?

Smiling with encouragement, her new friend reached over the console of her car and squeezed Amelia's wrist. "Don't be nervous, dear. Willow's looking forward to meeting you. And I don't live far away if ever you need me."

Humph. She'd gone from avoiding involvement with the locals to living minutes from a woman with whom she'd shared more about her personal life than she'd ever shared with anyone.

"Willow's roommate recently left town for college," Charlotte explained as they made their way along a pretty street of whitewashed homes with blue shutters and tubs of brightly coloured geraniums out front. Charlotte had told her the town, one hundred kilometres south of Sydney, had originally been settled by a Greek family. Twenty years ago, the name had changed from Little Parga to Water's Edge when a developer built a resort complex on the edge of town, but these Greek-style homes remained.

Perhaps Willow lived in one? That would be cool.

Charlotte turned a corner and stopped in front of a single-storey pale-blue weatherboard home. No geraniums, but the garden looked tidy and well maintained.

"Here we are."

Right. Her fidgety hands reached to toy with her silver rings

—rings she'd taken off never to put back on. Amelia gulped. "Can I have a smoke before we go in?"

She'd been trying to give up since she gathered smoking was one of those things frowned on in her new circle, but right now, she'd kill for a cigarette.

Charlotte smiled her understanding. "No problem, but how about we pray instead?"

Oh. She'd stuffed up again. How long would it take to get a handle on this? "Um. Okay." Amelia blew out a breath and tried to ignore the little voice that told her prayer wouldn't give her the same kick nicotine would.

Charlotte laid a hand on Amelia's. "Lord, I ask that You still Amelia's nerves. I understand how anxious she is meeting Willow. But, Lord, You can calm angry seas, and I know You can calm Amelia's heart. May she be aware of Your presence in her life, right here right now. In Jesus' precious name, I pray. Amen."

"Amen," Amelia echoed, feeling marginally more at ease. She got out of the car and followed Charlotte up the short path.

The door swung open before they had a chance to knock. "Hello! You must be Amelia!"

Well, duh. Yes. But goodness. Wearing a red polka-dot skirt and a crisp white-collared shirt, with a splash of freckles across her nose and a tanned complexion, the beaming woman should be on a fancy yacht, sailing the Pacific Ocean. Her lipstick was as bright as a cherry, and her curly blonde hair bounced on her shoulders.

Cringing, Amelia swiped a hand over her jean-clad thighs. Maybe she should have tucked in her T-shirt? At least it was clean and didn't smell of beer, but man, was she underdressed.

Despite her attire, the woman's contagious energy coaxed Amelia's lips into a smile. "And you must be Willow."

Willow threw up her hands and giggled. "Guilty as charged. Come in, come in!"

Okay...

Like her cheery host, the picture window invited the sun directly into the sitting area where it brightened up an overstuffed blue, velvet couch crowded with colourful cushions, two matching armchairs, and an oak coffee table. The baby-pink curtains matched the pink wall clock and the pink pots where thriving houseplants basked in those sunny rays on the windowsill.

She gestured to the couch. "Take a seat. I made us some lemonade." She chattered as she filled glasses from a paisley pitcher. "I was so excited when Charlotte told me about you."

Excited? She wouldn't be if she knew anything about her. They were utter opposites. Amelia doubted Willow had ever set foot into a bar or smoked a cigarette.

Amelia managed a smile. "It seems our shared need for a roommate came at the right time. Thanks for agreeing to meet a perfect stranger." Especially one like me.

Willow waved her off as she perched on an armchair. "Anyone who's a friend of Charlotte is a friend of mine." She grinned. "I have a feeling we're going to get along just great!"

Hmm. Amelia wasn't so sure.

Charlotte looked between her and Willow and nodded. "I agree, and for that reason, I'm going to take my leave and let you two get acquainted." After setting her empty glass on the side table, she pushed to her feet and rested a hand on Amelia's stiff shoulder. "I'll stop by later to help you move your things from your old place."

Assuming Willow agreed to her moving in. And that she accepted the offer. But then... what choice did she have? She needed to leave her old life behind, and that meant leaving the apartment that reeked of stale beer and cigarettes. Not that her roommates were bad, but their language was colourful and their morals questionable. According to Charlotte, to grow in the Lord Amelia needed to surround herself with like-minded people, people who loved the Lord and wanted to serve Him, because temptation would always be knocking on her door.

She swallowed hard and managed a smile. The woman's kindness was beyond measure. "Thanks for everything, Charlotte."

"You're more than welcome." Charlotte smiled as she leaned down and hugged her.

Being hugged, being looked after—it was all so new. How could people be so caring and kind?

After Charlotte left, a short awkward silence stretched on before Willow bounced to her feet. "I completely forgot! Would you like to see your room?"

Before Amelia had a chance to answer, Willow was off, beckoning her to follow through a kitchen as brightly lit and cheerful as the front room and down a narrow baby-blue hallway to the bedrooms.

"This one's mine." Beaming again—it seemed to be her natural state—she turned into a doorway on the left.

Amelia followed. Wow. The room matched Willow's style exactly. Pink curtains, a classy, black-and-white chequered bedspread, and pristine white furniture. Everything neat and tidy.

But then Amelia blinked. She edged closer to inspect a table tucked behind the door covered with messy scraps of colourful fabric with a sewing machine just visible beneath them.

"You sew?"

Willow edged up beside her and fingered one of the scraps. "I do. I'm working at Sarah's Waterside Coffee house to save money for fashion college. Between what I'm saving and what my parents are contributing, I should be able to start in a year's time without landing a heap of student debt."

"That's amazing. I'm impressed." No one Amelia knew had gone to college, let alone saved up for it.

"Thanks." Willow smoothed out the scrap she'd been fiddling with. "My sewing projects tend to take over, but I try to keep them contained to my bedroom as much as possible. Apart from occasionally needing you to model something, my obsession shouldn't disrupt your life too much." She let out a cheerful chuckle.

Charmed by Willow's fun-loving wit, Amelia laughed. "I'd be happy to assist."

"Great." Willow's eyes sparkled. She stepped out of the room and pushed open the door to the bedroom across the hall. "And this is your room."

That meant she'd passed, didn't it? A wave of emotion washed over Amelia. Clogged her throat.

She'd intended to haul in the air mattress she'd been sleeping on for over a year, but this room was furnished. A handmade patchwork quilt covered a single bed while a wooden desk nestled beneath the window and an old-fashioned wardrobe dominated the opposite wall. Amelia pushed back the tears stinging her eyes.

"It's all right, isn't it?" Willow's brow knit. "I know it's small."

Blinking back the tears, Amelia shook her head. "It's not too small. It's perfect. I–I was going to bring my air mattress."

Willow's eyes widened like she was trying to process that statement. She probably hadn't seen an air mattress. Maybe didn't even know what one was. "No need for that! Everything's here."

She crossed the room and opened the wood-slatted wardrobe door. "There's plenty of storage space above the clothes area if you want to store it."

Amelia shook her head. "No, it's time to get rid of it. I blow it up each night, and it's deflated by morning. It's time for it to go."

Willow's expression softened. "Charlotte told me you'd just left working at the bar. I'm glad you got out of there. Water's Edge has a lot of great places, but that's not one of them. It's not easy switching your job and living situation at the same time, so please know I'm here to support you in any way I can. After all, we're sisters now!"

"Sisters?"

Willow crossed the room and pulled her into a warm embrace. "Of course! Sisters in Christ."

That was a new one. As an only child, Amelia often wondered what it would be like to have a sister. She'd not expected one like Willow, but she was already warming to this vivacious blonde with her huge personality.

But as much as she wished to form a response, Amelia couldn't. It was all too much.

Willow clearly didn't mind as she fluttered around the rest of the house ensuring Amelia knew where everything was before they returned to the front room where she replenished their lemonade glasses and dropped back onto the snug couch, sunlight embracing her as one of its own. "Charlotte said you're going to start work at the diner. You'll love working for her."

"She's an amazing woman."

"Have you been a waitress before?"

Perched on the edge of the cushion—part of her still afraid she'd get something dirty—Amelia swirled the lemonade in her glass. "I've mostly done bartending, but I've waited tables, too. I was also a caregiver at an assisted living facility just after high school. But it wasn't for long, so that doesn't count."

Willow slapped the cushion beside her. "Of course, it counts! How did you like it?"

Amelia stared at her glass. Ran her finger down it, gathering up condensation. "I loved it, actually. I didn't expect I would. I'd heard the job was far from glamorous." She lifted her gaze. "That much was true, but something about helping people stuck with me, made me think working in that field could be rewarding."

Willow clasped her hands beneath her chin. "You should be a nurse!"

Amelia shrugged. "Yeah, I thought about that. But studying was never an option. I haven't stayed in one place long enough to make higher education practical."

"That's not to say you won't have an opportunity in the future." A soft blonde brow lifted as Willow cocked her head.

"You never know what sorts of opportunities the Lord will provide. Coming right out of high school, I thought pursuing a career in fashion and having my own boutique one day would be impossible since I didn't have the money." She waved a hand. "I didn't get a scholarship like my brother, and we were raised believing we shouldn't go into debt if we could help it. Even to study."

Amelia sucked in a sharp breath. "A scholarship, huh?"

"Yes." Willow's fondness for her brother became tangible as she went on. "For architecture. Lucas is a cool guy. You'll get to meet him on Sunday. He's the head of the worship team *and* also the youth pastor."

"Sounds like a busy man." But why wasn't he working as an architect if he'd gotten a scholarship in that field? It didn't make sense.

Before Amelia could ask, Willow reached out and gripped her arm, her eyes shining. "I just thought of something! You should join the Wednesday night Bible study. It's fantastic, and it'll be a great way for you to get to know like-minded people and study the Word at the same time."

Like-minded people. Christians. Amelia's heart swelled. This was a whole new world, and God had seen fit to supply her with friends like Charlotte and Willow to guide her down this amazing new path.

She smiled. "I'd like that. Thank you."

Chapter Two

With an absent-minded smile, Lucas Kelley oversaw the kids in the children's wing of Water's Edge Community Church in a rambunctious game of dodgeball. They'd been remarkably attentive during his teaching but had plenty of pent-up energy to expel. He would've been content to watch until every last one was collected, but he needed to get to the adult service to close in worship. Rarely was he assigned to both the children's wing and the worship team in one service, but today had gotten off to an unusual, yet exciting start. His fellow worship leader, Trish, had been assigned to the adult service but had gone into labour with her first child during the wee hours of the morning. As he made his way to the door, he offered a silent prayer for a smooth delivery of the congregation's newest member.

He'd just placed his hand on the doorknob when little feet scrambled behind him. He turned to find James, a five-year-old with thick auburn hair that now stuck out in every direction, beside him.

"Where are you going?" James asked, his face red.

Lucas ruffled the boy's wild hair, sweaty after his exertion in the game. "I need to go to the adult service now and lead worship."

"But you said you'd play dodgeball."

He knelt in front of the boy. "I know I did. I promise I will next week. Do you know why I need to go and help with the service?"

That hair bounced as James shook his head.

"Because Trish went into the hospital today to have her baby."

The boy's eyes lit. "You mean, when she comes to church next week, she'll have a *baby*?"

Lucas chuckled. "Yep, she sure will. In a couple of months' time, we might even get to have the baby here in the children's wing with us. When we do, you'll help look out for him or her, right?"

James's vigorous nod sent his hair flapping. "Of course, I will! I'll tell the baby all my dodgeball secrets so when he's older he'll be ready to play with me."

"That's a good man." Lucas clapped him on the shoulder. "You'd better get back in the game now. Your team needs you."

The little boy was quick to do as he was bade. Leaving the children in the capable hands of two older teens, Lucas made his way down the hall towards the main sanctuary, his step light. James's wonder over the start of new life resembled Lucas's awe a few years ago when he experienced new life of another type. The spiritual type.

Although raised in a Christian home by parents devoted to the Lord, he'd drifted from his faith during his early twenties, wandering from job to job and person to person in search of meaning and love, taking paths he'd be ashamed of to this day were he not keenly aware of God's abounding mercy. Regardless of how far he'd strayed and despite his stubborn rebellion, the Lord had brought him back into the fold, redirecting him to a better path. One filled with peace and purpose.

As he entered the sanctuary's back room, gratitude that His Saviour had seen fit to use a wayward man like himself for His purposes washed over him afresh.

Pastor Noah was wrapping up his sermon. Lucas's guitar was ready, propped against the dark wooden panelling of the backstage area alongside a pair of drumsticks.

"Here's our fearless leader." Adam March, the faithful keyboard player on the worship team for two years, greeted Lucas.

As he picked up his guitar, Lucas grinned at his friend. "You're too kind. Shall we?"

Joined by the drummer, Aaron Bates, they stepped onto the stage as a group. Compared to the city's megachurches, the Water's Edge congregation was small, but this was where Lucas's heart lay. Many worship leaders may have sought fulfillment in leading larger congregations, but he wouldn't trade these beloved faces for all the mega congregations in the world. This community had his heart.

As he took his place behind the microphone, his gaze landed on Willow. He gave his sister a quick smile, but then his gaze shifted to the young woman beside her. Charlotte had mentioned his sister had a new housemate. She'd omitted mentioning how attractive she was.

Pulling his thoughts back, he nodded to the others, and they began the introduction to one of his favourite worship songs, 'In Christ Alone'. As the words washed over his soul, he committed the coming week to the Lord. His hope truly was in Christ alone. Jesus was his light, his strength, and his song. He couldn't imagine living without Him.

When the praise time concluded and the service wrapped up, Pastor Noah approached and pumped Lucas's hand. "Thanks for stepping in at the last minute today."

"My pleasure," Lucas replied. "Any news on Trish?"

"Not yet, but I'm guessing any time now."

"Yeah." He had no idea how long these things took, but surely, the baby would come when it was good and ready.

"Regardless of when it arrives, Trish is going to be out of commission. We might've been tardy starting our search for her replacement."

Lucas waved off his words. "Don't worry. I'm happy to jump back and forth between the kids' wing and the adult service until we find someone to fill in."

Pastor Noah clapped him on the back. "Good man."

As Willow called Lucas's name, they both turned. When she beckoned them from the foot of the stage, they descended the platform steps to join her.

"You look as chipper as ever, Miss Willow," Pastor Noah complimented, squeezing her hand with grandfatherly affection. "Always a bright light on Sunday or any other day."

Willow's pretty pink blush matched her skirt. "Thank you,

Pastor Noah. I wanted to ask if there was any news about Trish."

Distracted by the young woman standing behind her looking painfully uncertain, Lucas didn't hear a word as Pastor Noah filled Willow in. Tall and slim, the newcomer flicked rich brown hair over one shoulder, letting it slink down the middle of her back. Even the fretful twist of her mouth couldn't hide the most perfect lips he'd ever seen. As she studied Willow, her dark-brown eyes mysteriously reticent, she seemed both reluctant and eager to join the conversation.

"Where are my manners?" Willow exclaimed. Reaching behind her, she coaxed the young woman forward. "Pastor Noah, Lucas, I'd like to introduce you to Amelia, my new roommate."

Smiling warmly, Pastor Noah extended his hand. "We're glad to have you here, Amelia. Welcome to Water's Edge Community Church."

"Thank you. It's good to be here." Her hesitant smile somehow matched the sincerity in her surprisingly strong voice.

Lucas reached out to shake her hand as the pastor left to speak with other members of the congregation. "You're a brave one to put up with this sister of mine."

Willow laughed and gave his arm a playful swat. "You mean because of my elaborate fashion ventures? I'll have you know Amelia said she'd be happy to help with them in any way she can."

Giving an exaggerated huff, he wagged a finger at Amelia. "I don't think you know what you've gotten yourself into."

"I'm grateful she's willing to rent a room to a stranger." She shrugged as though she wanted to say more but something stopped her.

His heart went out to her. Many a lost sheep had walked through those church doors—he'd been one not long ago. But her apparent struggle affected him. Her tangible desire to belong fought whatever was holding her back. What part of her past made her hesitant to embrace the church's warm welcome?

"Charlotte's given Amelia a job at the diner," Willow piped up, saving those around her from awkwardness in her usual way.

"That's great!" Lucas replied. "Make sure Charlotte puts you on Saturdays so you can meet everyone. Just about every single person in Water's Edge makes it to the diner for the lunch specials."

"So I've heard. I can't wait." That hesitant smile reappeared. It wasn't the first time the close-knit community where everyone knew everyone intimidated a newcomer.

He would have liked to chat further with Willow's new roommate, but the worship team clean-up couldn't wait. "If you ladies will excuse me, I'm on take-down duty. It was nice meeting you, Amelia."

She gave a nod. "And you, Lucas."

Willow flashed him a grin and then linked her arm through Amelia's. "I don't know about you, but I'm famished. What do you say we head to the store and grab some groceries to make our first gourmet Sunday lunch together in *our* kitchen?"

Visibly relaxing, Amelia smiled, his sister's inclusiveness once again working its magic. "Sounds great," he heard her say.

The two women exited the church arm-in-arm. Once they disappeared through the double doors, he made his way back to the stage.

. . .

Lucas arrived at his second-storey apartment late in the afternoon. He'd enjoyed lunch at the local seafood restaurant with some men from church, and then he'd driven along the ocean road with the canopy of his Triumph Stag down so he could both feel and breathe the refreshing sea air. There was nothing like it.

He made a point of carving out time on Sundays to regroup before the rush of day-to-day activities stole his peace. The beauty of the region, with its long sandy beaches and rugged clifftops provided the perfect setting for doing just that, but sometimes he wondered what it would be like to share the experience with someone special.

There hadn't been anyone for many years. Not since he'd ruined things with Carolyn. He didn't blame her for breaking it off. She deserved much better than the lost soul he'd become during his two years at uni. Although he was now trusting the Lord to bring someone special into his life, sometimes he wished He'd hurry up—after all, Lucas was more than ready.

Entering the kitchen, he tossed his keys onto the counter and opened the fridge. He groaned. Half a carton of eggs, two cans of soft drink, and a bottle of Tabasco. The sparse contents weren't the only evidence of his bachelor lifestyle. The walls were devoid of pictures, and mail littered the front room's coffee table that most women, especially his sister, would have tidied to make room for a stack of magazines and an assortment of other decorations.

He cracked open a can of Coke and headed for the couch, which contained neither a throw blanket nor a decorative pillow, while listening to the voicemail he'd missed. The message was from Finlay Walker, who was helping with the church's current building project, a Youth Centre Lucas was passionate about.

"Hey, Lucas. Just wanted to let you know a group of folks from a church plant in Sydney have agreed to come down and give a hand on the first day of building. Exciting, huh? We'll need all hands on deck to get this place built, but I know we're gonna do it. Talk soon, friend."

Lucas stared through the window at the darkening sky. His vision for a Youth Centre had been brewing for a long time. He dreamed of creating a space where the kids of Water's Edge could spend their free time playing games, attending Bible studies, and being mentored by people who cared deeply for them while forming meaningful friendships with their peers.

All too often in small towns like Water's Edge, young people grew tired of the close-knit, safe environment and ventured into the city where all sorts of trouble awaited them. It was his prayer and hope that having a supportive and fun space to hang out in might stop youth from straying out of boredom and encourage them to immerse themselves in the ways of the Lord during their formative years. The centre wouldn't be a complete fix for youthful rebellion, but it *would* provide a positive option.

With his experience in architecture, he was heading up the building project and loving every minute of it.

As he sipped his Coke, his thoughts strayed, yet again, to his sister's new roommate. She must be emerging from a rough past. Perhaps, if there'd been a place like this proposed Youth Centre when she'd needed support as a youngster, that pain might have been lessened or even avoided. He was only surmising, but the Lord had blessed him with not only a heart for the lost but also the ability to see below the surface. He didn't take his gift lightly.

Amelia was part of the Water's Edge community now, and they would care for her in the same way he wished to care for every kid who walked into the future Youth Centre—with kindness, gentleness, and compassion. Only God could heal her hurts, but they could show her loving acceptance. Wasn't that the great commandment? To love the Lord your God with all your heart, soul, and mind and to love your neighbour as yourself? Not an easy thing to do, but so worth it.

He finished his Coke and opened his computer. With two weeks before commencement day, he needed to go over the plans once more to remind himself it was happening because at times it felt too good to be true.

Chapter Three

Amelia's eyes widened when Willow pulled yet another stunning creation from her wardrobe—a velvet evening dress in the most gorgeous green. Stepping closer, Amelia ran her palm over the luxurious fabric. "It's beautiful. So soft."

"It's one of my favourites." Willow beamed. "Perfect for a night out in Sydney or a fancy dinner party with friends."

"I don't know how you do it."

Chuckling, Willow hung the garment on the wardrobe door. "I have excessive creative energy, I think. I was creating dress designs long before I could sew."

Amelia nodded to the sewing machine, a large black, apparently well-used, one. Ancient. "You sew everything on that?"

"It was my grandmother's. She helped me sew my first project on it. An apron."

"Do you still have it?"

"I do. It's in here somewhere." Willow rummaged through

her bottom drawer, then held up a small half-apron. "I was five when I made this."

"It's cute. I love the colour."

Willow seemed to tickle the ruffled edges as if coaxing a smile from a beloved infant. "I loved yellow when I was little."

Little wonder that such a ray of sunshine would be drawn to it. "It's a nice warm colour."

"It is, isn't it?" She returned the apron to the drawer and was pulling a blazer from her collection when the front door opened and closed.

"Anybody home?" a female voice called.

Willow tossed the blazer onto the bed and linked her arm through Amelia's. "That's my mum. Come and meet her!"

Having no choice but to comply, Amelia let Willow drag her out of the room.

In the hall, a middle-aged woman held a cloth-covered dish. Her lips, accentuated by bright pink lipstick, stretched into a broad smile, the soft blue of her eyes and her bouncy blonde hair giving away her connection to Willow. She winked. "I've invited myself to dinner since your father's tied up at church tonight. I hope you don't mind. I brought chicken stroganoff."

"Yum! Thanks, Mum. And of course, you're welcome." Willow kissed her on the cheek and accepted the dish. "Amelia, I'd like you to meet my mum, Sheila. Mum, this is Amelia."

Sheila stepped forward and gripped Amelia's hands. "I'm so pleased to meet you. I apologise for not being there on Sunday to greet you at church. My husband and I were picking up some things in Sydney for the Youth Centre."

"Did you get the pool table?" Willow asked.

"We sure did. And you won't believe what else. A brand-new volleyball net and ball."

Willow bounced like a little girl. If she hadn't been holding that dish, she'd likely have been clapping too. "Really?"

Sheila released her hold on Amelia and ushered her towards the kitchen. "The centre isn't built yet, so we have nowhere to put these things. But they were too great a deal to pass up. It was pick them up straightaway or lose them."

"Right." The Youth Centre was news to Amelia, but Willow and her mum seemed excited about it.

"I'm sure Lucas will know somewhere to keep them." Willow scooted ahead of them into the kitchen. "He has answers to most things. Anyway, let's eat before this gets cold." She placed the dish on the table while her mum got out the plates and cutlery.

Once they were seated, Willow held out her hands. "Shall we give thanks?"

For an instant, Amelia hesitated. This was all so new and unfamiliar like she'd gotten off a train and entered a whole new world, one where loving mothers dropped by with precooked meals and giving thanks was an everyday occurrence. It was weird, but kinda nice, like a cuddly blanket on a winter's day. Taking Willow's petite hand, Amelia closed her eyes and echoed the heartfelt thanks her friend offered to their Lord and Saviour.

When Willow pulled back the tin foil covering the casserole dish, tendrils of aromatic steam drifted Amelia's way, and her mouth watered.

All the while, Willow continued chatting about the centre as she served up.

"It sounds like a huge undertaking," Amelia remarked just for something to add to the conversation.

"It is, but it's going to be so worth it." Sheila poured iced tea from a mason jar into three tall glasses. "We need all the help we can get. You should get involved, Amelia. It's going to be an exciting project to be a part of."

"Mum, I already roped her into Wednesday night Bible study. We shouldn't bombard her with too many things too soon."

"Of course. I'm sorry. You've a great deal going on with moving and starting a new job."

Shelia had that right. Amelia still couldn't believe everything that had happened. "It's been hectic, but thanks for inviting me. I'll keep it in mind." A lump had formed in her stomach. How could she become part of a community like this? These people were so nice. She wasn't worthy to serve alongside them. They'd see right through her. Her sins were forgiven, but would she ever feel good enough to mix with such perfect people?

Every bit of her felt deflated, but then she recalled a verse from the Bible study the night before. *Therefore, if anyone is in Christ, the new creation has come: The old has gone, the new is here!*

She *was* a new creation. Her old self was gone, so there was no reason she couldn't fit in. Still, it was easier said than done. What would Sheila think if Amelia uttered a swear word or lit up a cigarette? How long would it take her old habits to die?

As Willow and Sheila chatted happily, Amelia did her best to join in. They got on so well. So different to her and her mum. Not that they'd seen each other lately. Or spoken.

When the food had been devoured and the dishes cleared, Sheila took her leave, hugging Willow and then Amelia, promising to come to the diner before the week was through to say hello.

"Your mum's a lot like you," Amelia remarked after she left. "You must have gotten your hospitality gene from her."

Willow rolled her twinkling eyes. "Yeah, Mum makes it her mission to get everyone involved in everything. Community is her passion." Then her brow lowered. "I hope you didn't feel pressured when she mentioned volunteering for the Youth Centre project."

Amelia opened the tap and started filling the sink with warm sudsy water. "Of course not. I appreciated her including me. It's just..." Her voice caught. Could she open up with Willow? Share things she'd never shared with anyone? Even Charlotte?

When she glanced back at Willow, her roommate was studying her.

Sighing, Amelia turned off the tap, dried her hands on a towel, and leaned against the sink. "Can I share something with you?"

Willow's expression softened. "Of course."

Despite her roommate's open expression, Amelia's heart pounded. This type of vulnerability was new to her, but it was the way forward—wasn't it? She pushed out a long breath, imagining pushing out her insecurities as well. She could do this. With her gaze low, she began. "Charlotte told you a bit about my past."

"She did. I hope you don't mind."

How *could* she mind? "It's only fair since we're sharing a house. That you knew about me but still welcomed me with open arms means the world to me." Amelia swallowed, hardly able to believe she was doing this. "But I'm scared others won't be so understanding. Since I left home when I was seventeen, I've been searching for meaning and purpose. That search led me down paths I'm not proud of." The lump clogged her throat again, so she swallowed harder. But it came right back as she recalled some of the nights when she was so off her face she had no idea who she'd slept with. Nor how many. Her stomach twisted, heat washed over her, and something prickled behind her eyes. Would those memories ever leave her?

"I–I knew they weren't great choices, but I didn't know where to turn." The smile she forced tasted sour, bitter, something she didn't want anywhere near her lips. "I look at this beautiful community of believers who've been so kind to me, and I can't help wondering if they'd see me differently if they knew my past. I can't help feeling unworthy around such people."

"Oh, sweetie." Willow stepped forward and squeezed her hand. "Every believer in our church—in the whole world, in fact —has one thing in common. We're *all* sinners, washed by the blood of Jesus. Forgiven. We all struggle with sin and need to be forgiven daily. No believer is any better than any other. We've all done things we're not proud of, so you're not alone."

That might be true, but she doubted they'd done the stuff she'd done. Alcohol, drugs, sex... At least she hadn't gotten pregnant.

Her throat was too tight to speak.

"If it's of any help"—Willow fixed a button coming undone on her crisp white blouse—"the welcome you've received from everyone is one hundred percent genuine. There's no need to be afraid of getting to know them or of allowing them to get to know you."

A tiny flame of hope flickered. *Could* Amelia stop running? Have a place she could call home amongst people who knew and cared about her without judging her? It felt impossible, but maybe, just maybe. She gave a tentative smile. "Okay. I'm not sure, but I'll try. I promise."

"Good girl." Willow pulled her in for a hug. "This is just the start of your journey. No one's judging you. We're all just happy that God brought you here."

Tears stung Amelia's eyes. What had she done to deserve such a kind friend? "Thank you." She sniffed. "I'm glad, too."

Willow grabbed a tissue and handed it to her. "Dry those eyes and let me finish those dishes. Don't you have an early start in the morning?"

Amelia accepted the tissue and glanced at the clock. "I'm opening with Charlotte. She wants me to learn the early-bird schedule, and then I'll be fully trained."

"So quickly!" Willow's eyes lit up. "You're clearly a fast learner."

Amelia waved off the comment. "I'm not so sure about that. I still feel more at home pouring beer than making coffee. I never knew how hard it is to make the perfect cup."

"I'm sure you'll get the hang of it soon enough."

"I hope so. Anyway, thank you again. For everything."

"You're more than welcome. Sleep well."

With the bed so soft, it would be hard to do anything but. She gave Willow a warm smile. "I'll do my best."

As she refilled coffee cups for three kindly grey-haired gentlemen who'd sat at the same table closest to the corner window every day that week, Amelia couldn't help but smile. Instead of serving disorderly intoxicated men, she now served war vets, sweet ladies out for their weekly girls' brunch, and young families with children who took joy in drawing and colouring at the tables while they waited for their meals.

In the homey, wholesome atmosphere, with sunlight flowing in the windows, waves tumbling onto the shore, and flowers cheering up each table, the distrust and peril that always lurked in her previous workplaces seemed a world away.

The leader of the Wednesday night Bible study, a man named Adam, had said every good and perfect gift came from above. She could hardly believe the gifts the Lord had bestowed upon her. She didn't deserve them, but man, was she grateful to have left her old life behind. Although she still hungered for a cigarette at each break.

The men thanked her, and she headed back to the counter to refill the pot. It was crazy how much coffee the customers drank.

"How are we doing?" With her cheeks flushed from the morning rush, Charlotte proved she might be the boss, but she worked as hard as her employees.

"Pretty good," Amelia answered. "I was about to put on more coffee."

Charlotte swiped a cloth down the counter. "I knew you'd be great at this job. You fit right in, luv."

As much as she appreciated the words, Amelia wished they were true. Her last attempt at creating a fancy pattern on a cappuccino hadn't gone well. Instead of looking like a heart, it resembled an alien from outer space. Seriously, *how* did the other girls get their designs to look so perfect? For now, she'd stick with filtered coffee. She could do that.

When the bell over the door jingled, she looked up. Willow had mentioned dropping in for a coffee, so Amelia had been half expecting her. She hadn't mentioned Lucas would be coming with her.

Butterflies took flight in Amelia's stomach. Willow's good-looking brother had been at the Bible study, and during their brief awkward conversation, she'd been keenly aware of his bright blue eyes, his strong stature, and his distracting dimple. She couldn't remember the last time she'd felt so inept around a man. And now she'd have to serve him coffee. Great.

She was acting like a silly schoolgirl. If she could handle intoxicated men ogling her, she could deal with a squeaky-clean, blue-eyed youth pastor. Even if the mere look of him did strange things to her insides.

Pasting on a smile, she grabbed menus. "Hey, Willow, Lucas. Great to see you!"

Willow sniffed the breakfast-scented air. "I came to see *you*, but now I'm here, I can't pass on a double serving of blueberry-stuffed French toast!"

Chuckling, Amelia gestured towards an empty booth near the front windows. With the ocean shimmering below and a light sea breeze, it was the perfect spot for her new bestie and her brother. "We can take care of that. Right this way."

As Lucas passed, his smile made her pulse skitter. She swallowed hard. What *was* she doing? It was stupid. He was a friendly man. He'd smile that way at everyone. Stop being so twitterpated.

"Can I get you some drinks to start?" she asked after they were seated, her voice sounding more normal than she'd expected.

"Do you know what I've been craving?" Lucas leaned back against the seat and folded his arms. For a youth pastor, he sure had some muscles. Not that she was looking.

"The blueberry-stuffed French toast, of course." Willow pointed at that item on the menu.

"No. A thick chocolate malt with extra cream. I don't suppose you could muster one of those up, could you?"

Amelia gulped. "Sure. No problem." It had to be easy, right? "And, Willow, coffee?"

"Yes, please. A cappuccino would be lovely."

Amelia hid her groan. "Coming right up."

At the counter, she proceeded to make the thick shake with Charlotte's help.

"Lucas likes his shakes extra thick and creamy," her boss said. "He's got a bit of a sweet tooth."

"Right." Something to tuck away.

Charlotte added chocolate shavings and a cherry. "There. Just the way he likes it."

"Now I need to do Willow's cappuccino. Can you show me again how to do the heart?"

"Sure."

She made it look so easy. Amelia ground her teeth. One of these days, she *would* get the hang of it.

With a beverage in each hand, she headed back to the booth, determined not to allow Lucas to affect her. But her resolve to escape the uncharacteristic girlish butterflies vanished the moment he spoke. How did he do that?

"I can safely say that's the fanciest thick shake I've ever been served here. Charlotte didn't tell me she'd hired a decorator for a waitress."

Heat crept up Amelia's neck. What was going on? Had Charlotte set her up? "Charlotte helped me make it."

"Did she just?" His mouth quirking, he sipped from the straw.

"She said that's how you like it."

"With a cherry on top?" His brow lifted.

She nodded. She'd have to have words with Charlotte. Surely her boss wasn't trying to matchmake? How could she ever think she'd be a suitable match for someone like Lucas?

"It's fine. I like cherries on top." He winked, and the heat reached her cheeks. Was he flirting?

She wished he'd break eye contact, but he continued to smile. "Charlotte was lucky to find someone like you. You're obviously a great asset."

"And she's a great roommate," Willow piped up. "Now, let's get our food orders in. I'm wasting away here."

Thank goodness for Willow. Her words saved Amelia from further discomfort.

"Right." She grabbed the notepad and pencil from her apron pocket. "French toast for Willow. And what can I get you, Lucas?" She pinned him with her gaze. *If* he was flirting, he'd met his match. He had no idea how many men she'd put in their place over the years. But, oh goodness! He was different from the men she was used to. She could easily fall for him if she wasn't careful.

She jotted down his order of steak and eggs and returned to the kitchen to tack the order page up where the chefs would see it. She then busied herself with replenishing the napkin dispensers lined up on the counter.

"How did Lucas like his thick shake?" Charlotte flashed a playful grin.

"He loved it."

"Good." Yep, no missing the knowing expression Charlotte sent her way. "He's a nice young man, isn't he?"

Amelia paid more attention to situating the napkins than was necessary. "He is."

"I'm sure you'll get to know him now you're rooming with Willow." Charlotte patted her arm before dashing off to attend customers.

Amelia exhaled. As much as she'd like to know Lucas better, she would keep a proper distance.

It was for the best.

She wouldn't lose her heart to that too-handsome youth pastor sitting in the booth, although she couldn't help glancing his way as she went to greet the customers who'd just stepped through the door.

Chapter Four

The rest of the week passed quickly. Charlotte gave her plenty of work, and when they were both home, Amelia spent hours with Willow talking about faith and reading the Word. Amelia had so many questions and was so hungry to know more about this new life she'd embarked on.

She was coming to accept that God loved her, warts and all. He no longer saw the mistakes of her past—her sins had been dealt with on the cross. That blew her away.

At church on Sunday, she determined to focus on God and not on the youth pastor, although it was easier said than done since she could see one and not the other. But she came away uplifted by the message and the worship and only a little annoyed that, when Lucas spoke to her after the service, her pulse had skittered.

During the Wednesday night Bible study, she exchanged friendly greetings with the folks she'd met the previous week.

She was growing more at ease and not so concerned with what people might think of her.

After helping themselves to the pot of steaming coffee and delectable croissants, she and Willow settled into chairs at the round table in the prayer room off the main sanctuary. She couldn't help glancing around for Lucas. Disappointment weighed down on her. He wasn't here. Maybe he wasn't coming this week.

Intent on focusing on the study, she pulled out her Bible and the notebook and pen Charlotte had gifted her. That was, after all, why she was here. She scooted back in her stiff chair. Cosy couches lined the pale-lemon walls, and a welcoming fireplace lent a homey feel to the prayer room.

"I'm super excited for this study." Willow nudged her with her shoulder. "I loved what Adam talked about last week."

The topic of being free in Christ had stuck with Amelia throughout the week as well. In the past, she'd viewed church as a restrictive establishment—one that gave the people within it a list of don'ts to abide by. But when Adam spoke on Romans chapter eight, verses one and two, she'd realised how deeply she'd misunderstood the statutes of the Bible. The concept that the law of the Spirit provided freedom from the bonds of sin and death was mind-blowing and left her eager to hear more.

"Welcome, everyone." Adam, who looked to be in his thirties, greeted the group with a friendly smile and glowing brown eyes as he settled down at the table, a cup of coffee in one hand and a Bible with a worn cover in the other. "Let's get started, shall we?"

As they opened in prayer, Lucas entered the room. Her

heart fluttered, and she groaned. How did he manage to do that to her?

"Hey, Lucas. We're only just starting." Adam waved him in as the attendees turned in their Bibles to the passage for the evening.

Lucas retrieved his Bible from the spot at the table he'd clearly reserved earlier. "I've just come to grab my stuff, actually. Turns out, they're short-staffed in the kids' wing, so I'll be in there tonight and not here. Sorry."

As he scanned the room and their gazes met, Amelia wondered if his flash of interest was real or imagined. Ugh. Why couldn't she ignore him? Why was she allowing herself to think about him in that way?

"There for our kiddos, as always." Adam rubbed his clean-shaven jaw, one brow rising towards his dark hair. "Do you have enough help?"

Lucas raked a hand through his trim brown hair. "We're still short a person, but we'll make do."

Though she wasn't sure what possessed her, Amelia spoke up. "I can help."

She gulped as their attention focused on her. What *had* she done? If only the floor would open up and swallow her.

"That's so nice of you." Willow squeezed her hand, her eyes wide as if she, too, was wondering what had possessed her.

Tucking a strand of loose hair behind her ears, Amelia sent Lucas an uncertain smile. It was too late to retract her offer, wasn't it? "I–I mean, only if you need it. I love kids." Well, she thought she did. She'd never really had anything to do with them, but she'd always thought working with kids would be fun. Better than working in a bar, anyway.

"If you're up for it, I'd be more than grateful," he answered. "But only if you want to."

Heart thudding, she nodded. "I–I want to."

"Thanks, Amelia." Adam slapped the table. "You'll have a great time. The kids are a riot. In the best sense, of course."

Good-natured laughter from the room's occupants followed his statement as she gathered her belongings, still wondering what had possessed her. Had she gone insane?

"I know you were looking forward to the study tonight," Willow said. "But don't worry. I'll catch you up. Go have fun with the kiddos."

"Thanks." Hugging her new Bible to her chest, Amelia headed to the door.

When Lucas smiled warmly as they exited the room, her face burned. He must have thought her offer presumptuous, but there was no going back.

Walking beside him to the kids' wing, she was careful not to look at him, although she was aware of him. How could she not be? He walked with a spring to his step and radiated an almost-magnetic vitality.

"Thanks for volunteering, Amelia."

"You're welcome. I haven't hung out with kids in a long time, so it'll be fun." That was true. It *had* been a long time since she'd hung out with kids. Like about twenty years. When she was a kid herself.

"There aren't too many. Just the kids of the parents and the office staff attending the study. Still, we like to have two people on duty at all times."

"That makes sense."

As they rounded a corner and children's voices reached her

ears, her hands grew clammy. She didn't have the first clue what to do with them.

"Ready to enter the mayhem?" Lucas joked.

She managed a smile. "Yes."

Stepping into the room, she narrowly missed a dodgeball to the head, ducking just in time.

Mayhem, indeed. She picked up the ball as a little boy with wild auburn hair raced forward to claim it, his arms outstretched. "That's mine, lady."

"James, let's remember our manners," Lucas admonished, grinning. "Try 'I'm sorry, Amelia.'"

Amelia did her best to hide her mirth as James turned his flushed face upwards.

"I'm sorry, Am—e—a." He could barely say her name.

"It's quite all right, James. No harm done." The moment she handed him back the ball, he was off.

Lucas's fondness for the child glowed on his face as he watched the boy race back to the game.

"Managed to round up reinforcements, huh?"

Amelia swung around. "Charlotte! I didn't know you were here."

"I'm not usually," her boss explained. "I came by to drop off some pastries for you all to enjoy during the study and heard they were short-staffed over here with the kiddos. I offered to watch them until Lucas returned."

There was no missing Charlotte's approval as her gaze shifted between her and Lucas. "I'd love to stay and help. But I have to get pie crusts going, or Water's Edge will be short on sweets tomorrow."

"Thanks so much, Charlotte." Lucas gave her a friendly smile. "But between us, we've got it under control."

Amelia chewed her bottom lip. *He* might have it under control.

"I can see you do. Well, catch you both later." Charlotte winked before breezing out of the wing.

As warmth crept up her neck again, Amelia huffed out a long breath. She needed to forget any romantic notions and focus on the kids. That's what she was here for, after all. But it didn't help that Lucas looked so hot. And cute.

Oh...

To take her mind off him, she scanned the room. A loaded bookshelf took up one corner, along with a mat before a whiteboard. The kids' backpacks hung on a row of hooks on the opposite wall. Colourful covers of children's Bibles peeked out of the half-zipped packs. Upbeat music played from a nearby sound system.

Lucas glanced at his watch. "Time to round 'em up and start the service."

Service? The *kids* had a service?

He grabbed hold of a megaphone and put it to his mouth. "All right, y'all, time to wrap up the ball game and get ready for lesson time. I'm starting the clean-up timer now. Go!" He grinned at her and tapped his watch. "Their record is forty-seven seconds for having the whole place tidy. Well, nearly, anyway."

"Forty-seven seconds." She arched a brow and shook her hair over one shoulder. "Not bad."

Sure enough, every child in the room was seated on the mat in record time.

"What was our time, Lucas?" asked a pigtailed girl, her hazel eyes huge.

Lucas's face shone. "You beat your record, guys! Forty-five seconds."

Cheers rose around the group. Amelia couldn't wipe the smile off her face even if she tried. The ease with which he wrangled their boisterous energy and got the kids focused on the lesson was nothing short of miraculous.

He leaned towards them, suddenly serious. "Can I tell you a secret?"

Their eyes grew wide as their heads bobbed in eager nods.

"When I come in here to teach you kids, I learn more from you than you do from me."

"But you're the teacher!" James piped up.

Lucas shrugged. "I know, but sometimes, I feel like the roles are swapped. Jesus made it clear that we adults have a lot to learn from kids. You have such a special way of seeing things that the God of the universe made a point of telling us adults to learn from your faith. That's cool, isn't it?"

Amelia settled in a nearby chair, as fully enraptured as the kids while Lucas launched into his teaching on having childlike faith. Much as she'd been looking forward to attending the adult Bible study, she soon realised *this* was where she needed to be. There was no shame in being at a 'young' stage in her faith. As long as she remained deeply rooted in a community that put the Lord first and sought Him, she would grow, just as these children would.

By the time Lucas wrapped up the teaching, she knew he could have managed the kids alone with no trouble at all. They loved him and gave him their undivided attention.

He picked up his guitar. "Who's ready for a song?"

Once again, enthusiasm rang out all around. The teaching had been impactful, but the worship that followed was even more so. Awestruck, Amelia hugged her arms to her body as the children showed why God called His people to consider the example of the young. Their joy was contagious and genuine, and tears sprung to her eyes as they sang.

But more than the children captured her attention. Whether he was under the sanctuary stage lights singing into a microphone with a band behind him or seated on the floor in front of kids, Lucas's heart for worship burned brightly. Before coming to Christ, she'd wondered why people sang in church. After this, she'd never wonder again. The life breathed into the room by complete focus on God and His goodness in song gave her the answer.

By the time he wrapped up the service with a prayer and released the kids to continue their dodgeball game until their parents came for them, her heart was overflowing.

He set his guitar down and joined her. "Thanks again for jumping in at the last minute."

She was quick to wave off his words. "It was my pleasure. I probably got more out of the service than the kids."

His brows rose. "You too?"

She nodded. "Charlotte and I talked about childlike faith and having complete trust in God, but the way you presented it made total sense."

"I'm glad." His expression softened. "The Lord works in mysterious ways, doesn't He? I learned a long time ago that I need to be in here breaking down His teaching for the young because it helps me as much as it helps them."

They turned back to watch the kids playing their game. She wouldn't soon forget this impromptu venture into the children's wing and the renewal it brought to her soul. Or the radiance on Lucas's face as he led the children in praise. He was like an angel—not that she knew what one looked like—but she could almost imagine a halo above his head.

Could you fall in love with an angel? She wasn't sure, but if she wasn't careful, she could fall for Lucas, youth pastor or not.

Chapter Five

Directly after wrapping up worship team practice, Lucas headed for Dr. Samuel Turner's office. He and Water's Edge's one and only doctor were scheduled to discuss details about Saturday, the day construction on the Youth Centre would begin. The elderly doctor had offered to organise the volunteer help, from refreshment committees to first aid.

Lucas had just fired up his Stag when his phone rang. Since it was Willow, he quickly accepted the call. "Hey, Sis. To what do I owe this pleasant surprise?"

"Lucas. Thank goodness you answered!"

His sister's panicked voice caused his grip to tighten on the phone. His breath whooshed out with the words, "Is something wrong?"

"She was up on the step ladder outside, and she fell. Her ankle's hurt."

"Slow down. Who fell? Amelia?"

"Yes! She can't walk. Can you come?"

"Of course. Be there in five." He did a quick Uey and headed to his sister's, praying the injury wasn't serious. If it were, she would have called the ambulance, right? For some reason, though, his sister believed he could fix anything.

At the house, Amelia and Willow were seated on the front porch, Amelia holding an ice pack to her ankle, her face pale. Willow was rubbing her housemate's back.

"This doesn't look like fun." Lucas crouched down to inspect the ankle. Not that he was a doctor. Or even versed in first aid. "What happened? When Willow and I were in for breakfast yesterday, you were buzzing around the diner with such ease, and now here you are, an invalid."

Amelia pressed a hand to her forehead. "I was going to water the hanging plants on the porch, so I got on the step ladder. I should have taken them down and then watered them, but I was tall enough to reach. I rolled my ankle when I went up on tiptoe and fell."

"I think we'd best get you to the doctor." He wasn't sure, but it could be broken. Hoping he was wrong, he slipped his arm around her waist and helped her up. "Put your arm around my shoulders, Amelia. Willow, go to her other side."

His sister nodded and complied, her face ghastly white.

"We'll get you to my car and take you to Dr. Turner. Let us take your weight, okay?"

"Okay." Amelia's voice was little, and she winced as they took the first step.

"Would you like me to carry you?"

She shook her head. "I'll be all right. I'm sorry to be a bother."

"Gracious, Amelia, you're hurt!" Willow exclaimed. "You're no bother."

"It was such a stupid accident."

They reached the passenger side of the car. Willow opened the door while Lucas lifted Amelia in with one swift movement. She was such a slight thing. "Don't worry. We'll be there in no time."

As he slipped into the driver's seat and Willow squeezed into the back, Amelia folded her hands in her lap and looked at him. "I hope I'm not making you late for anything."

Her vulnerable uncertainty stirred something in his heart. He swallowed hard. "Nope. I was headed to Dr. Turner's office anyway, so it's no trouble at all. But even if I'd had other plans, this would have taken precedence."

As he smiled at her, he wondered at the strange stirrings in his chest. Could this young woman be the one he'd been waiting for? Something about her drew him. She was attractive, but it wasn't that. The depth to her intrigued him. He wouldn't mind digging to discover what lay beneath the surface. If she'd let him.

Starting the engine, he engaged first gear and gripped the steering wheel. It had been a long time since a pretty girl sat beside him. When he glanced at her from the corner of his eye, a smile lifted his lips, and an almost imperceptible tingle ran through him.

Minutes later, Willow leaned forward and squeezed Amelia's shoulder. "We're almost there. I'll run in and get Dr. Turner. Lucas can help you out of the car."

At the medical centre's car park, Willow was busting to get

out, but with the canopy down and only two front doors, he had to get out first. "Hold your horses, Sis."

When he opened his door and climbed out, Willow scrambled out behind him and dashed inside while he hurried around to help Amelia.

She looked up, her brown eyes soft. "I should be able to walk with a bit of help."

"Don't be silly. I can carry you."

"I don't want to be a bother."

Was she erecting a wall, or was she used to fending for herself? Probably both. "You're not a bother."

She swivelled around and shuffled to the edge of the seat. When she placed her uninjured foot on the ground, he bent down and helped her up, supporting her weight until she steadied herself.

"Take it nice and slow."

As her arm settled around his shoulders, he breathed in the scent of her freshly washed hair, and his heart flip-flopped. Not since Carolyn had a woman touched his heart in this way. But was she interested? He'd thought so, but now he wasn't sure. Shaking his head, he helped her inside. No time to ponder matters of the heart now.

"Hello." Samuel crossed the room, his gaze fixed on Amelia. "I'd heard there was a newcomer in town. I'm sorry we're meeting under these circumstances. I'm Dr. Turner, and you must be Amelia."

She nodded, but a grimace twisted her lips. "Yes. Nice to meet you."

"Let's get you to the exam room. Willow, grab a wheelchair from the back room. That's a dear."

With a nod, Willow dashed to the back of the surgery, returning seconds later.

"Let's ease you into it. Lucas, would you help me lower Amelia? Amelia. A pretty name for a pretty girl."

Lucas grinned. The good doc had a knack for calming his patients. Guess it came with years of practice.

They eased her into the chair, but pain still etched her face. He squeezed her shoulder. "The doc will look after you."

She looked up and gave a hesitant nod.

He remained with Willow in the waiting room after Samuel wheeled Amelia away. His sister nibbled her nails. "This is terrible. She could have done without this."

"She'll be all right. It's most likely only a sprain." Although he wasn't convinced. If Amelia's pain was any indication, it could be a lot worse. "Why don't you settle down and find something to read?"

"How can I sit still while Amelia's in there?" Willow began pacing as the minutes ticked by.

By the time she agreed to sit, Samuel had returned. She jumped back to her feet.

"How is she, doc? Is it broken?"

He gripped her shoulders, the corners of his eyes crinkling. "Goodness, Willow, you're more worked up than you were when you and your parents brought ten-year-old Lucas into my office with strep throat."

Willow glanced sheepishly at Lucas. "A kid at school told me you'd never talk again and your tongue might fall off. Of course, I was worried."

The memory provided a dose of much-needed comic relief.

When they'd finished chuckling, Lucas spoke. "How *is* she, doc?"

"With a few days' rest, she'll be as good as new."

"It's not broken?" Willow's eyes glistened.

"No. Just a bad sprain. You can go see her if you like. I've applied an ice pack to bring the swelling down. She's resting for a bit."

Willow didn't need to be told twice. She dashed into the treatment room.

Relieved, Lucas turned to the doctor. "Would now be a good time to have that chat?"

"Sure. I'll grab my notes."

He disappeared into his room and returned carrying a notebook. Sitting beside Lucas, he flipped it open and cast his gaze down the page. "Most bases are covered. Mr. and Mrs. Miller agreed to manage the cold refreshments, and Jonny's manning the playground so volunteering parents don't need to worry about watching their kids."

"That's great." It was all coming together. *Thank You, Lord.*

The doctor's brow lowered, and he rubbed his jaw. "I thought there was one more slot to fill, but I can't seem to remember what it is."

"I'm sure it'll come to you. Anything to do with the food?"

"No. Charlotte's overseeing the potluck, and your mum's looking after the tea and coffee."

"Of course."

"Lucas, can you come help Amelia?" Willow called from the exam room.

"Sure." He pushed to his feet, and Samuel did likewise. "Let me know when you remember what it was," Lucas said as they headed to the exam room.

He could hear Amelia's protests before he even entered the room.

"Really, Willow, I've inconvenienced your brother enough already."

"You heard what he said. He was coming here to see the doc, so you didn't inconvenience him at all. Besides, you're hurt. There's nothing wrong with accepting a little help."

"She's right." Lucas stepped into the room. "You didn't inconvenience me."

When both women swung their gazes to him, he gulped. What was it about Amelia that did strange things to his insides?

She shook her head. "I don't want to sound ungrateful. It's just Willow was going to ask you to take me home, but there's no need."

"And how else do you expect to get home? Wheelchair?"

Her chin jutted. "I can call a taxi."

He stifled a chuckle. "You'll do no such thing. I'm happy to help. In fact, I *insist* you allow me to take you home. Plus, I can't leave Willow stranded."

Her back straightened, and her chin jutted further.

He groaned. Was she pushing him away, or was she being independent? She was used to looking after herself. Most likely, after living that way for a long time, she found it hard to accept help. He could understand that. Perhaps that was it. She wasn't pushing him away on purpose. She just didn't know how to let people in. Which was puzzling after her eagerness to help with the kids the other evening.

He softened his tone. "Besides, Dr. Turner and I just finished our discussion, so I was ready to head out."

"First aid!"

Everyone's attention turned to the doctor.

"The last slot we need to fill is another first aid volunteer."

Willow jumped in. "Amelia used to be a caregiver, and she's been thinking about going to nursing school. Why don't you have her on the first aid committee?"

Amelia's jaw dropped. "I'm *not* thinking about going to nursing school. I just worked in an aged care home for a while, that's all."

Samuel faced her. "But you know some first aid? We could use your help if you're up to it." His eyes crinkled up again. "Probably doesn't seem fair, does it? You come in with an injury and go out committed to a favour."

Grimacing, Willow ran a hand over her hair. "I was just telling you not to feel pressured, and here I am suggesting another volunteer opportunity. I'm sorry." She plunked down and took Amelia's hand. "But it does seem to be a perfect fit. Something you'd enjoy."

Amelia released a breath. "It's not that I don't want to help. I did do a first aid course." She lifted her gaze and shrugged. "It's just that I was a caregiver for such a short time, and it was so long ago...."

Samuel was already waving away her protest. "Nonsense. Anyone who's worked in an assisted living facility is more than qualified for what we'll need. It's a precaution, really. We're not anticipating anyone needing medical aid, and of course, I'll be around. So, what do you say? Can we count you in?"

She looked to Willow before her gaze swung to Lucas as if seeking confirmation.

He gave an encouraging nod. He had no idea she'd done anything other than wait tables or serve behind a bar, so learning she'd worked as a caregiver, even for a short time, was enlightening.

"Okay." She faced the doc. "As long as you're sure you want me. Besides, I couldn't do much else with this ankle."

"Excellent! And yes, you're right. We'll set you up with a chair and a footstool to keep it elevated, although by Saturday you should be walking on it a little. Now, let's get you into Lucas's car so you can get home and put it up. Don't forget to do that. It's important."

"I won't. And thank you again."

Samuel smiled. "You're more than welcome. And welcome to Water's Edge, Amelia. I hope you feel at home here."

"Thank you. It's starting to feel like home."

"That's good to hear."

It *was* good to hear. Lucas sensed she'd been running for some time. Running from what, he wasn't sure, but perhaps the Lord had brought her to Water's Edge for a reason. Salvation, for one, but perhaps... He gulped. He was getting ahead of himself. She'd given no indication she even liked him. In fact, her reactions indicated the opposite.

But maybe that was her protecting herself.

He was getting the feeling there was a side to Amelia Anderson she hadn't allowed him—or anybody—to see, but underneath her layers of protection she had a caring heart. While having breakfast at the diner the previous day, he'd observed her interactions with the other customers. She was attentive and gracious. Some might say it was the usual enthusiasm demonstrated by a new hire, but it was more than that. Unless she was an accomplished actor and fooling everyone, she cared about people.

And that thrilled him.

As he helped her out the door, he found it impossible to harness his racing thoughts.

Let alone his heart.

Chapter Six

Arriving at the Youth Centre construction site with Willow three days later, Amelia leaned against the passenger seat and released a breath. The centre was being built at the back of the church. Willow had told her they'd bought the ocean-facing block of land when the house there was put up for sale. The house had been knocked down, and now, construction on the Youth Centre was starting. From the number of people buzzing around, everyone seemed keen to help with the huge undertaking. And therein lay the problem.

Everyone was too helpful. Too kind. She'd walked into some kind of Utopia where nothing ever went wrong and people smiled all day. That wasn't the world she came from. It seemed less than real. Did they never have problems?

Willow claimed God gave His children strength to handle whatever problems came their way, but He didn't always prevent them. Amelia hadn't seen any problems, but maybe it was true. Perhaps they had them, but they smiled anyway.

"Hey." Willow's bouncy hair fluffed around her face as she turned to Amelia. "Are you okay?"

When Amelia had shared some of her concerns and even tried to back out of helping today, Willow had insisted she come. "You can't let Dr. Turner down. He's relying on you."

Yeah, right. He said he'd be around. He didn't need her. He was trying to include her. They all were. And here she was. She ran her finger through her hair, catching on a snarl. "I guess so."

Willow grasped her hand and squeezed in an achingly sweet bestie's kind of way. "You'll be fine. Let's go find Dr. Turner and get you set up. Okay?"

Amelia relented with a tight nod. "Sure." Freeing her hand from that too dear gesture, she swung her legs out of Willow's car and grabbed the crutches the doctor had given her. She could do without them. But her ankle was still sore, and he'd told her it was better to use them, even though they were a pain.

They found the doctor in the kitchen chatting and sipping coffee with Charlotte.

"Hey, look who's here!" Charlotte's eyes lit up as she hugged Amelia.

Goodness. Would she ever get used to this?

"How's your ankle?"

Amelia shrugged. "It's okay." She felt terrible about letting Charlotte down. "I should be back at work next week."

The doctor raised his brow. "I'm not so sure about that."

"I've been staying off it as much as possible."

"I'll check it later, but right now, let's set you up with your kit. I'll go grab it."

She let out a breath. "Okay."

Moments later, he returned with a first aid kit and a lanyard stating her position as a medical volunteer.

"Like I said, God willing, we won't need to employ your skills today, but stay alert because you never know." He clapped a man of a similar age to himself on his back. "Stuart, here, is your offsider. He's a qualified first aider, so together you should be fine, but call me if you need help."

"Nice to meet you, Amelia." Stuart extended his hand. "Sorry to hear about your injury."

She fumbled with the crutch and managed to get her hand out. "Thank you. It's almost better. I might ditch these when the doc's not looking."

"You'll be in trouble." His grey eyes twinkled.

"Oh well." She was used to trouble. What was new?

"Would you like a coffee? Something to eat? I can bring it over. Our station's just over there." He pointed to a table on the side wall surrounded by plastic chairs.

"That would be nice, thank you. I'll go put my foot up. Best do what I'm told. Don't want to upset the doctor."

"Good girl. I'll be right over."

She offered a smile and hobbled to the table. Through the window, she could see all the outdoor activity and the glistening ocean beyond it. What a perfect setting. Much better than the western suburbs of Sydney where she'd grown up. Her heart skipped a beat as she sighted Lucas wearing an orange high-vis long-sleeved shirt, khaki work shorts, and boots. So different to his church attire, the outfit suited him. Gave him a manly look. Not that he didn't look manly normally.

Ugh. What was she doing? She let out a sigh as she eased her foot onto the cushioned chair. She was deluding herself if she thought he might be interested in her. Besides, they were such opposites. He was squeaky clean. She was tainted.

Stuart arrived with a plate of yummy pastries and fruit and two mugs of coffee. "I wasn't sure how you like it, so I brought extra sugar."

"Thanks. I take it how it comes."

"Too easy." He sat down and took a bite of a Danish. "These are great. You should try one."

She chuckled. "I know how good they are. Charlotte makes them for the diner."

"Oh, that's right. You work there."

"I do. Not that I've worked lately." She swung her gaze to her ankle and rolled her eyes.

As they continued chatting, she kept glancing out the window. She couldn't help it. The Lucas magnet drew her gaze. It didn't matter where he was—up a ladder, down a hole, behind a crowd—her gaze found him, and her pulse kicked up a notch. It was stupid. She knew that. But she couldn't deny his appeal. He was such a hottie.

He looked as much at ease in the position of project manager as he did on the church stage leading worship. As he interacted, he doled out that smile that had tied her feelings into knots back at the diner and then again in Dr. Turner's office.

Confirmation that his kindnesses to her weren't anything special.

She was simply another member of his beloved congregation.

That was all.

All morning, the only call for first aid help was a teenage girl who'd gotten a splinter while helping carry some timber. It was an easy fix, and Stuart had it out in no time. Then he left her to speak with his wife who was helping in the kitchen. It seemed every family had contributed to the potluck lunch. As the salty ocean breeze played with red-and-white gingham tablecloths over the long tables, casseroles, pasta salads, fruit bowls, and a delectable selection of pies anchored the coverings in place.

Amelia's stomach was growling before Willow arrived. "Come on. Time to eat. We do it in shifts. We need to get in before the men. Otherwise, there won't be anything left."

"Oh. Okay." Amelia grabbed her crutches and hobbled to the table.

"You've got to try Mauve's redskin potato salad." Willow picked up two paper plates and heaped a serving of the salad onto one.

Apparently, Amelia was having it whether she wanted it or not. But it did look good. "It's a winner, huh?"

Willow motioned her hand outwards, kissing the air in classic Italian fashion. "Magnifico."

"Well, if I'm having potato salad, I'll have to pair it with a piece of that fried chicken."

"Mrs. Granger's specialty." Willow waved a hand over the spread. "You can learn about each woman in this town by looking at this table. Pretty cool, huh?"

"It is." It was more than cool. Amelia hadn't experienced an event like this before. She'd been to group functions, of course, but never one that harboured such a genuine sense of community.

Willow chose a Mexican pie and added some to Amelia's plate before they made their way to a picnic table near the playground where the children were chasing one another, their happy squeals ringing out.

"How's your ankle?" Willow asked as she dug into the pie.

"Much better. Although I wish it hadn't happened. I feel so stupid."

Willow fingered flyaway strands of bouncy blonde hair away from her face. "Perhaps it was providential."

Huh? Amelia angled her head. "What does that mean?"

"Sorry. I shouldn't talk in jargon. My bad. It just means that perhaps God allowed it to happen for a reason."

"Like what?" Amelia picked up a piece of chicken.

"Well, you got to help out here, and you talked to Dr. Turner about your interest in nursing. You never know what might come of that."

Amelia snickered. "That was thanks to you. Besides, this is just a volunteer opportunity, not an acceptance into nursing school."

With her blue eyes alight, Willow's expression remained hopeful. "Small steps in the right direction. You should seriously think about pursuing your dream."

Appealing as the idea sounded, Amelia couldn't help but hesitate. She was getting used to a complete life change and the Lord had blessed her greatly on her new path. Hoping for even more when so much had already been given seemed unreasonable. One glance at Willow showed her friend had guessed her train of thought.

Pursing her lips, Willow sent her a stern look. "Nothing happens without it first passing across God's desk. Perhaps there was a reason you toppled off that stepladder. Don't underestimate what could come from it, okay?"

Amelia cocked her brow. She doubted anything would, but she wouldn't argue. "Okay. I'll keep it in mind."

"Something sure smells good over here."

Her heart jolted as they both looked up. Lucas was approaching the table, although she didn't need to look up to know that. She would know his smooth, deep, confident voice anywhere. Somehow, it managed to slide under her skin and wrap around her heart.

If only there was food on her plate to distract her, but she'd finished it all.

There was no option but to look at him.

His steady gaze was already fixed on her. "How's our injured warrior doing today?"

Gulping, she tucked a strand of hair behind her ear. "I wouldn't say I'm much of a warrior, but it's feeling better today, thank you."

"Glad to hear it." He leaned over his sister's shoulder and inspected the pie left on her plate. "Mmm. Smells good. I'd better get some for myself."

"Do," Willow encouraged. "And once you have, come back and sit with us."

He glanced again at Amelia. "I believe I will. Be right back."

There was no missing Willow's pleased expression as he strode towards the table. "He likes you, you know."

Amelia's mouth went dry. She cleared her throat. A glass of water would be good right now. Or a cigarette. "No, he doesn't."

Willow crossed her arms and raised a quizzical brow. "You think I don't know my brother?"

"That's not what I'm saying." Amelia exhaled. "It's just that he's nice to everyone."

Willow shook her head. "This is different. Trust me."

"He's an attractive man. He probably has all the women of Water's Edge wrapped around his finger."

Willow's gaze swung to him. He was chatting with a group of teens while piling his plate with food. "You're right. Plenty of girls like him and would fall over themselves to date him, but he hasn't dated anyone for years. He doesn't bestow his interest lightly, so believe me when I tell you I know when he's interested in someone."

Amelia gulped again.

Before she had a chance to respond, he joined them. Her pulse took off when he sat across from her with one of his smiles.

Maybe he *did* like her.

"The ladies sure outdid themselves this time," he said while digging in.

"You all deserve it for working so hard." Jumping to her feet, Willow motioned to the adjoining car park where a car had just pulled in. "Looks like Charlotte's arrived with fresh coffee. I'll go help her. Talk amongst yourselves."

Great. She and Lucas were on their own.

Amelia cleared her throat. No need to act like a tongue-tied fool, although a family of butterflies had taken residence in her stomach. "So, how's the building going? It seems like you're making good progress."

He surveyed the volunteers who were still working. "If there's anything this town knows how to do, it's pull together for a good cause. And cook."

She chuckled. "That's for sure." She hesitated before continuing. "Willow told me you studied architecture—received a scholarship, in fact."

"Ha. Willow, the chatterbox." He speared a piece of rockmelon with his fork and then grew serious. "I did study architecture for a time, but I didn't finish the course."

"Why not? That is, if you don't mind my asking." Perhaps he wouldn't like her prying.

"Not at all. I stopped because I realised it wasn't my true calling."

She tipped her head to one side, trying to make sense of that. Even if it wasn't her calling, if someone had offered her a scholarship, she would have snatched it with both hands. "But if you received a scholarship, you were clearly gifted. How did you know it wasn't your calling?"

His gaze shifted to the kids playing tag. As he studied them, she found it hard to breathe, so when he spoke, she was grateful she didn't have to talk.

"I'd done almost two years of the course when I was invited to serve as the youth pastor here. At first, I wasn't sure I should be entrusted with guiding young minds. It's such a responsibility." He paused before his lips lifted. "I prayed about it, and I came to believe it was what God wanted. So I quit the course, and here I am. I love being a worship leader, but I've truly learned more from working with the kids."

Despite the intensity of his eyes, she managed to put aside her previous awkwardness and enjoy the conversation. "I'm sure it's fulfilling. That's a big life change, though—a complete redirection."

Thoughtfulness settled in the slight creases around his eyes and between his brows. "That's often what God does, if we're open to Him. We make our plans, but He determines our steps. Often that's not what we had in mind for ourselves, but it's always the best way, although it can take time to recognise that. Sometimes it's immediate."

"And was yours? Immediate, I mean."

"It was. A lot of folks didn't agree with my decision to leave uni. In fact, they thought I'd lost my marbles. But I'd talked to the Lord, and we were on the same page. So I went ahead, confident I was doing what He wanted."

Wow. Could God give her the assurance she needed to follow His plans for her life, whatever they might be? She silently prayed He would.

She was about to remark on how fortunate the community was to have his architectural expertise for the Youth Centre project when a scream came from the playground.

She shot to her feet. A little boy had fallen from a tree and lay on his back. Without any thought about her crutches, she hobbled to him. Lucas was right beside her, keeping one hand on her elbow to steady her until they arrived at the boy's side. Despite the adrenaline pumping through her veins, she couldn't ignore the warmth spreading up her arm at Lucas's touch.

The boy's playmates, whose faces displayed their worry, stepped aside as she settled on the grass. The boy lay on his side, crying. "It's all right," she cooed as she placed a gentle hand on his shoulder. "Can you tell me where it hurts...?" She looked to Lucas.

"Ezekiel," he supplied.

"Ezekiel. Can you tell me where it hurts?"

The boy, maybe eight or nine years old, blinked up at her and snuffled. "My a–arm."

Nodding, she faced Lucas. "You'd better find Dr. Turner and Ezekiel's parents."

"Of course." He was already on his feet.

She turned back to the boy. "Looks like you took a pretty bad tumble, young man."

"I–I was climbing that tree."

"So I see."

When he began crying again, her heart went out to him. He seemed in a lot of pain. She prayed it wasn't serious.

Not wanting to move him until Dr. Turner arrived, she settled for stroking his mop of brown hair. "Lucas has gone to find the doctor and your parents. What if I sing to you while we wait? Would you like that?"

He nodded. Hiccups had set in.

After thinking, she began singing 'Amazing Grace', the only hymn she knew all the words to. She'd sung others since arriving in Water's Edge but didn't know the words. It didn't matter. 'Amazing Grace' held so much meaning. The song might have been meant for Ezekiel, but the words washed over her soul afresh.

> "Amazing Grace, how sweet the sound
> That saved a wretch like me
> I once was lost but now am found
> Was blind but now I see."

By the time Lucas returned with Dr. Turner and Ezekiel's mother, Amelia was completely absorbed. With her eyes closed, soothing the boy's brow, neither she nor Ezekiel noticed their presence until she finished the final note.

"You've done a great job soothing the patient." His expression warm, Dr. Turner settled next to the little boy.

His mother's eyes were moist as she knelt too. "Are you all right, honey?"

He braved a small nod, but pain still etched his face.

She touched Amelia's shoulder as Dr. Turner began his examination. "Thank you for comforting him. I'm so glad you were here."

Amelia shrugged. "It was nothing, really. I'm sure he's not badly hurt, but I wanted to keep him calm until we knew for certain."

"I appreciate that." The mother swiped tears from her cheeks and extended her hand. "I'm Martha, by the way."

Amelia took it. "Amelia."

"Well, young man, nothing's broken," Dr. Turner announced. "Your shoulder will be bruised, but other than that, you're fine."

Martha gathered her son into her arms. "Thank you, Doctor. I'll take him with me. How does some cold lemonade sound, Zeke?"

The boy's eyes lit.

Something warmed inside Amelia. If only everything could be fixed with cold lemonade.

It wasn't until she stood that she noticed the way Lucas was regarding her.

She frowned. "Are you okay?"

He cleared his throat and ran his hand along the back of his neck, but a faint redness tinged his cheeks. "Y—yes, I'm fine. It's just..."

She raised her brows, inviting him to continue. How strange to be on the other side of the discomfort! What was going on with him?

"You have a great voice, Amelia."

She blinked. Really? Now it was her turn to blush. "Thank you."

"Has no one ever told you that?"

"Not really. It's good enough to impress on karaoke night, but..." She ducked her head, hoping to gloss over this reference to her past.

"It's much better than that. You have a real gift."

A gift? No way.

The cool she'd managed to maintain evaporated. Growing self-conscious and twitterpated once more, she twiddled a lock of hair. "I'm not so sure, but thank you." She glanced back at Ezekiel, half-hoping to use him as a distraction, but he was already headed towards the refreshment table with his mother on one side and Dr. Turner on the other. With no choice, she turned back to Lucas. "I appreciate the compliment."

He continued his thoughtful inspection. "Would you consider singing with the worship team?"

"You mean...?" She blinked. "At church?"

He rerolled the sleeve on his high-vis shirt. "You'd be doing me a favour because the woman who leads with me has gone on maternity leave sooner than expected. If what I just heard is any kind of a sample, the congregation would be blessed by your voice. You must have sung before. In school, perhaps?"

A dry laugh hurt her throat. "You wouldn't be caught dead singing in the schools I went to."

Oh dear. She'd let even more out without thinking.

"Well, whether you've sung before or not, we could use you on the team. What do you say?" He angled his head and held her gaze. "First Dr. Turner offers you a position as a first aid volunteer, and now I'm roping you into helping with the church service. You're being given jobs left, right, and centre. I hope you don't feel we're taking advantage of your talents."

"Of course not." She rubbed her arms. Not that she was cold "I'm honoured you'd think to ask me. It's just... I've not done it before, so I'm not entirely sure about it. I mean, I don't know that I deserve to..."

"Let me assure you. From what I heard, your voice is more than good enough."

He'd missed her meaning.

"There's no need to decide now, but after hearing you, I had to extend the offer."

What could she say? Goodness. It was all a bit much. "Can I think about it for a day or two?"

"Why don't you stop by the church on Monday when you finish your shift, and we can sing a few notes together and see how it goes?"

How could she refuse, especially when he was looking at her like that? She locked her hands together in front of her. "Sounds good, but leave it with me?"

He inclined his head. "Sure. No problem."

She expected him to walk away. Her heart skipped a beat

when he placed his hand on her shoulder. "Sharing your God-given gift isn't prideful, if that's what you're thinking. The Lord gives us those gifts for a reason."

Her mouth dropped open. Before she could reply, one of the volunteers called for Lucas.

"Looks like I've shirked my duties long enough. See you later?"

She blew out a long breath as he walked away. *Had* he invited her to join the worship team? He had no idea her hesitancy wasn't because she believed her voice to be inadequate but because she believed herself to be inadequate. What would he think if he knew her past? Discreet as Charlotte and Willow had been, it was only a matter of time before folks found out. Surely Lucas would agree that, even though God had forgiven her, she was a less-than-ideal candidate for such a role.

Still, Willow's words lingered in her mind: 'We all need forgiveness'.

Exhaling, Amelia hobbled back to the first aid table. Each person was gifted for a reason, Lucas had said.

Would she ever feel free enough to use hers?

Chapter Seven

Having completed her first shift back at work, Amelia tugged off her apron as she stepped outside. One glance at her watch confirmed her fear. She might be too late to catch Lucas. During the busy afternoon shift, she'd decided to meet him at the church to try out a few songs—after all, there was nothing to lose by doing so.

She quickened her pace while wrinkling her nose. The scent of burgers and fries clung to her clothes, and grease stained her shirt. Since she hadn't expected to talk herself into going to the informal audition, she hadn't had the foresight to bring a change of clothes, and with so many customers arriving before closing, she'd left the diner later than expected since Charlotte was never one to turn folks away. After being off work for so long, she'd been glad to stay and help—she still had rent to pay, after all. Going home now to change would make her even later, so she had to stick with what she had on.

As she passed the bar, familiar sounds drifted out. Called to her. The hum of men chatting. The clink of glass. Jukebox music. The smells, too, were familiar. Beer, tobacco, old carpet. Although she had a new life, she'd still kill for a cigarette.

Lord, give me strength to walk on. To choose You. To leave my old life in the past, where it belongs.

She crossed the road and, stopping outside the church, checked her reflection in one of the windows. Even after she adjusted her ponytail and smoothed her shirt, her appearance was far from polished. Like she had any reason to care what Lucas thought. Rolling her eyes, she made her way inside,

The moment she set foot in the sanctuary, her nicotine craving and thoughts of her outfit vanished. The reverent atmosphere enveloped her like a warm fire on a rainy day. Cosying into the peace, she breathed in deeply to draw as much of it into her being as possible while the dim lights cast shadows over the pews, giving her the urge to slip into their seclusion and pray alone, just her and Jesus.

Music floated to the ceiling. With him unaware that he was no longer alone, Lucas's hands continued their skilful movement over the keys of the grand piano. She should alert him to her presence, but unable to bring herself to do so, she sank into a pew near the front to listen. She didn't know he played.

Though he didn't sing, she recognised the melody of 'Come Thou Fount', a worship song they'd sung at church just the day before. Tears sprang to her eyes as the verses came to mind and she considered how she'd grown in the Lord during her short time in Water's Edge. And yet, there hadn't been a moment more poignant than the one she now experienced as the

Father's love wrapped around her heart and gave more comfort than she'd ever experienced.

She listened until the final note, her eyes remaining closed even after the music ended. They flew open when she remembered Lucas's presence.

He was angled towards her on the piano bench, his gaze steady, warm.

She brushed the tears from her cheeks, laughing. "I'm sorry..."

He stood, picked up a tissue box from behind the lectern, and joined her.

"What are you sorry for?" His voice soft, he eased onto the pew beside her and handed over the box.

Dabbing her eyes, she shrugged. "For sneaking up on you. And for crying."

With his sleeves rolled up, he rested his forearms on the pew in front. "I don't mind you sneaking up on me. As for the tears, I'm not *that* good a piano player."

"But you are." Sniffing, she let her smile wobble away. "You know, when you told me you'd given up architecture to devote your life to the church, I couldn't quite understand it. I think I do now."

He tipped his head. "And why's that?"

She motioned to the piano. "What you did... here alone, just you and God. You're truly His instrument."

His head dipped, his eyes hooded. "Thank you."

A short silence elapsed before he stood. "You're here, so I take it you're ready to try your hand at employing your God-given gifts."

She gulped. *Did* she have God-given gifts? What a crazy

thought. Hadn't He already given her enough by giving her new life?

She pushed to her feet, and her heart pounded hard as she followed Lucas to the piano. Would she be able to sing a single note?

He sat on the bench and motioned for her to stand beside him. "What if we start with 'Amazing Grace'? We can move on to other hymns after that. Sound okay?"

Nodding, she inhaled deeply.

When he began playing, she closed her eyes. As the melody reached deep inside her, her voice lifted—and she was transported to another time. Another place. Willow had told her that often happened during worship. It was like being in the very presence of God.

At the end, Lucas moved on to another hymn, 'How Great Thou Art'. She opened her eyes and read the lyrics as she sang. He sang with her, and she grew comfortable with the tune. As their voices blended, she grew more confident.

After a few more songs, he sat back and faced her. "Your voice is amazing, Amelia. Truly God-given. I hope you'll join the team."

A heavy breath slid loose. Could she? *Could* she join the worship team? Her heart was back to pounding. "I'd–I'd like to..."

His brow lowered. "You don't seem sure."

"I'm not." She rubbed her neck.

"What's holding you back?"

She felt vulnerable, but his sincerity gave her the bravery to answer. "I–I don't know how much Willow told you about my past."

He studied her intently. "Nothing. Your past isn't my business."

That seemed hard to believe since he and Willow were so close, but whatever. She took a deep breath and tapped her fingers on her leg. "I grew up in a rough household. My parents fought when I was young, and their marriage was always on the verge of collapse. I never knew what I'd come home to."

"I'm so sorry."

That wasn't the part she needed to tell him. She shrugged. "It's okay. I couldn't wait to leave, though. I thought striking out on my own would give me the stability, meaning, and purpose I hadn't found during my childhood. I left when I was seventeen and tried lots of things. I got involved in the party scene and all that comes with it." She closed her eyes as if she could shut out the memories. Memories she'd rather not have. Drawing another deep breath, she pushed on. "I drifted from town to town and took whatever jobs I could find. Mostly bartending."

A shudder worked its way up her spine. "I was good at my job and needed to make a living, but I grew increasingly disgusted by the degradation I felt from my bosses and the men I served liquor to. Nothing I tried and no one I reached out to brought me the peace and meaning I sought."

She faced him. She expected to see censure, but instead, compassion peered back at her.

"I'd just arrived in Water's Edge and had begun working at the bar when I met Charlotte. I was standing outside after fleeing a man who'd made inappropriate moves on me, trying to get myself together when she invited me to church."

One corner of Lucas's mouth tipped upwards. "That sounds like Charlotte."

Her gaze lifted to the gorgeous stained-glass windows surrounding them as she thought back on her first night within the church walls. "I was profoundly touched that night. The prayer for forgiveness and salvation she led me in changed my life. That was my final night bartending."

"So, you came to work at the diner."

She nodded. "And live with Willow and join the church." She slid a finger along the piano's glossy black surface. "Do you see now why I'm reluctant to become involved? Sitting in the pews and attending Bible study is one thing, but leading worship?" She crossed her arms over her chest as if she could protect her heart. "I'm not qualified. Not with the kind of past I've had."

He inhaled deeply and looked into her eyes. "I understand where you're coming from."

Of course he did. "I'm sure you've had others come to you for counsel."

"That's not what I mean. I understand because, not so long ago, I was right where you are now."

What? Her eyes widened. "You?"

He raked his fingers through his hair and let out a small chuckle. "Youth pastor, worship leader... I know it's hard to believe."

He had that right. "You're such a godly upstanding man. I was sure you'd been involved with the church your entire life."

He shifted along the piano bench and tapped the space alongside him, inviting her to join him. Though distracted by his woodsy aftershave and his close presence, she listened attentively.

"It's true. I was raised in a godly household. You've met my parents, so there's no need to tell you they're remarkable and God-fearing people. But, like you, I found myself searching for my own sense of meaning. That search sent my feet travelling down paths they oughtn't to have been on. Only by God's grace am I where I am today. You wouldn't recognise Lucas Kelley if you saw him four years ago."

He had to be joking. Lucas Kelley? Off the rails? She stared at him. "I had no idea...."

He laughed before growing serious again. "Our God is called a Redeemer for a reason. He redeems us because we can't redeem ourselves. When you come on Sunday, look around. Every believer has some sin in his or her past that's a source of shame, but each of those sins has been forgiven, the penalty paid by the blood of Jesus. I punished myself for years for the sins I'd committed, but then I came to accept that, when God sent His Son to die on the cross, the penalty for those sins was paid in full. We're all qualified in the Father's eyes. Even you. Even me."

He half-smiled, half-frowned, and as the truth sank into her soul, remarkable peace came over her. She'd heard it before, but this time, it reached deep inside her. Touched her heart. Her soul. "Thank you for sharing."

He reached out and squeezed her hand with the utmost tenderness. "And thank you for sharing both your story and your voice with me today."

It was just a friendly gesture, but his hand on hers was warm and kind. Never had she felt this much at ease with a man. She ached to turn her hand and clasp her fingers to his as she savoured the precious rest and safety she experienced in his presence.

A companionable silence fell before they both cleared their throats and stood, but then, with uncertainty squinching his eyes, he opened his arms. "A hug?"

A hug? Oh goodness. But nodding, she stepped forward.

Closing her eyes, she enjoyed the sensation of his strong arms around her. The scent of his cologne. The sound of his heartbeat.

They embraced for a long moment before separating.

"I'll take this to mean you'll join us on Sunday?" His head angled as his hopeful gaze held hers.

Her heart swelled. "Yes, I'll be there."

Chapter Eight

Picking one Saturday each month to hold a game night had been a Kelley tradition since Lucas and Willow moved out and started their own lives. Though they still lived close enough to their parents to visit often, such visits tended to get lost in the hustle and bustle of obligations, work, and friends. The game night ensured that, no matter how busy things got, the entire family had a chance to connect. They always selected a day that worked for *everyone*.

Lucas arrived home from a Youth Centre committee meeting just in time to change his shirt and grab the guacamole and chips from the kitchen before heading to his parents' house. Willow was in charge of the game selection this month, so he expected nothing less than a hilarious evening.

Her white Toyota Prius was already parked in the driveway. As he slipped off his shoes, the delicious aroma of homemade margarita pizza wafted through the open front door and made his stomach rumble. "Anybody home?"

"In the living room, honey," his mum called.

He dropped the guacamole off in the refrigerator and peeked into the oven at the pizzas before joining his family. He began talking as he approached the living room. "Willow, if you intend to beat me in Scrabble tonight, it's not happening. I'm feeling lucky, and I think..." His voice trailed off as he entered the room. Amelia? No one told him she was coming.

Seated cross-legged on the floor setting up the Monopoly board, she looked up with a shy smile.

Aware that his emotions over her presence were clear to all, he cleared his throat. "Hi. Come to join the party?"

"I hope I'm not crashing family night." She met his gaze before lowering her lashes. She was wearing denim overalls and a white T-shirt, and her hair, loose and hanging over her shoulders, looked freshly washed. The sight of her did strange things to his insides.

"Of course not." There was no one he'd be more thrilled to have join them. But one glance at Willow and then his mum confirmed his suspicions: the women in his life were getting ideas. As much as the thought of getting to know Amelia excited him, jumping into a tight-knit community was new for her, and the last thing he wanted to do was overwhelm her. Playing it cool was the only way to go.

"Did you bring the guacamole, Lucas?" Willow asked, already hard at work organising the bank.

He stood in the doorway and folded his arms. "Sure did."

"Good," his mother piped up. "Why don't you bring it out here as an appetiser while we wait for the pizza?" She patted Amelia's denim-clad knee. "Wait until you try Lucas's famous guacamole. It's his specialty."

"It's his specialty because it's the only thing he can make." Willow shook her head in mock despair as she sorted out the final stack of starting money. "He needs a wife. Badly."

Heat crept up his neck. What were they doing? What would Amelia think? He should scold them both right there and then. But Amelia's lips had quirked into an amused grin as she set out the chance and community chest cards. When she looked up, once again, their gazes met. She shrugged.

Perhaps she wasn't as embarrassed as he was. She'd worked in bars and handled all sorts, after all.

"I'll leave you ladies to talk amongst yourselves about potential improvements to my domestic situation while I grab my humble offering from the kitchen." He raised a brow at Willow and gave her a long glare as he exited the room.

Distracted by Amelia's unexpected presence, he almost bumped into his father coming out of the kitchen. "Hey, Lucas. Ready for Monopoly?"

"Always." He squeezed past him and pulled the guacamole from the fridge.

His dad leaned against the doorway, arms crossed. "I'm glad Amelia's joining us tonight. Did you know she was coming?"

Not his dad, too? He gave an offhanded shrug. "Nope."

"She's a nice young woman. I heard she's joining the worship team. That's good news."

"It sure is. She'll be a great addition."

"Come on. Let's go." Dad nodded towards the living room. "And don't worry. I'll make sure your mum and sister take it easy on you tonight."

Lucas's brows rose. "You mean, in Monopoly?"

Dad laughed. "Nah, you can hold your own in the game. But

the plan the two of them seem to be hatching might be another matter entirely."

Lucas stared after his father as he made his way into the living room. Seemed his entire family had it in for him. They could matchmake as much as they wanted, but nothing would happen unless Amelia was open to any advancement *and* he'd received God's green light, ultimately the most important consideration. So far, he had neither.

Inhaling deeply, he joined his family. And Amelia.

Willow rubbed her hands together. "All right. Let's get this tournament started."

"So, it's not just a game, but a tournament now?" He placed the guacamole and chips on the coffee table before taking the conveniently available spot on the ground beside Amelia.

"While you were out of the room, Willow told me about your Monopoly skill. When I said I wasn't too shabby at the game myself, she insisted we make tonight's game the first of a series."

"Hmm. She's that certain this friendly game is going to turn into an epic battle of skill, is she?" He lifted a brow as he positioned his legs under the table.

"Seems that way."

He levelled Amelia with a serious look. "Tell me honestly, should I be afraid?"

Her teasing expression made his heart somersault. "We shall see."

She had a competitive streak. He liked that.

"You'll have to show Amelia that, although your culinary skills are lacking, you excel in the realm of competitive Monopoly," Willow chimed in.

His gaze swung back to Amelia to gauge her reaction to the outright matchmaking.

Her expression mischievous, she gathered up her stack of notes. "I have a feeling he'll give me a run for my money. But I'm ready."

Kinda impressive how easily she'd settled in. Keeping his heart in check during the evening was going to be harder than expected.

Amelia was indeed an excellent player. By the end of the game, they were the last two standing.

He sat back, eyeing her appreciatively when she won. "You weren't kidding about knowing your stuff. Looks like it's you and me for the next round."

"You're on." She flipped her hair off her face. She had the biggest smile he'd ever seen, and she'd let it out tonight when she'd grown at ease during the game, joking around as if she were a family member.

"We'll keep you in the loop about the date for the next game night so you can have your rematch." His dad gave her a fatherly pat on the shoulder before stifling a yawn. "Well, I'm going to leave the rest of the evening to you young folks. It's time for me to turn in. After helping Mum with the dishes, of course."

Mum waved off his offer as she and Willow gathered the pizza plates and iced tea glasses. "We've got it handled, Mike. You've had a long day. I'm surprised you made it through the game."

He laughed. "Me too. All right then, I'll say goodnight. Thanks for joining us, Amelia."

"Thanks for having me." Pushing to her feet, she began helping with the dishes as he left the room.

"We've got it, Amelia." Willow smiled. "You're a guest. There's not much here anyhow. Why don't you and Lucas go out onto the porch and check out the moon? It's supposed to be full tonight, you know."

Really? Lucas glared at her. Not that checking out the moon with Amelia wasn't appealing....

"Some fresh air sounds nice," she said. "I'll grab another glass of iced tea to take with me. Would you like one, Lucas?"

He blinked. How could she be so calm? Maybe his turmoil wasn't evident either as he gave a nod. "That'd be great. Thanks."

His mother's approval was unmistakable as Amelia strode to the kitchen. When he crossed his arms and shook his head at his mother, her grin widened.

Willow waggled her eyebrows as she breezed past, so he glared at her again.

Before he could collect his thoughts or have words with the pair, Amelia returned with two glasses of tea.

"Ready?" She looked at him and then glanced between Willow and his mother. "What have I missed?"

"Er, nothing." He took his glass and led her out the front door.

The cool evening greeted them, along with a breathtaking sky atwinkle with stars strewn across it like fairy dust. Far enough away, the lights of Sydney were no match for the natural illumination in the heavens. Just as Willow had said, a large full moon hung low on the horizon and cast a shimmer across the sea, completing the picture.

They stood together on the porch, Amelia's closeness making his pulse quicken. His unspoken feelings for her were intensifying, but could he say anything? Was it too soon?

"What does your dad do for a living?" she asked, breaking the silence.

"He's an auto mechanic." He set his glass on the railing. "Best one around."

"I bet he taught you a thing or two about cars." She swung her gaze to him. "So, you can do more than just sing and teach kids and build things and make guacamole."

Loving the teasing lilt in her voice, he played along. "He taught me some. I mean, a guy has to know how to do at least a couple of things, right?"

She tucked wisps of hair behind her ears, her eyes shining. "I hate to say it, but I don't think you've acquired enough skills at this stage. But you still have time."

What stage was she talking about? Was she stirring, following the same vein as his sister and mother, or did she mean...? He swallowed hard. "I–I guess so."

They grinned at each other before turning back to the view. His parents, who'd worked hard all their lives, had struggled to scrape up enough money to buy the house when Water's Edge was a backwater. Now it was worth millions because of the town's proximity to Sydney and because it had one of the best ocean views in the area.

"My dad knows a lot about acquiring numerous skills," Lucas remarked. "He's been working day and night to help get the Youth Centre on its feet. He puts in so many hours helping me and the crew out that I often wonder how he has time to work in the shop."

"Your family's amazing, Lucas." Her wistfulness tugged at his heart. "I already loved Willow, and I'd met your mum and thought she was great.... But seeing you all together—your parents especially—blows me away."

Never would he take his parents' relationship for granted again. Nor his close-knit family. "When I was a kid, I didn't appreciate the strength of their relationship. Not until recently did I realise how special and rare it is."

He studied her profile. She looked more at peace now than when she'd arrived in town. Still, the depth of her thoughts and the hurts and disappointment beneath her surface pulled at him. He continued, hoping their conversation would encourage her to share even more.

"Although I had my parents as role models throughout my childhood, I didn't understand the value of a God-centred relationship until I experienced a few bad ones for myself."

Her brow rose ever so slightly.

"I don't mind talking about them," he continued. "If we can't learn from our mistakes, what good are they?"

A green tree frog began croaking.

Her expression thoughtful, she ran her finger along the condensation gathering on the side of her iced tea glass. "Perhaps you're right."

When she lifted her gaze to his, he leaned against the railing and looked into her eyes. His heart turned over at the openness he saw there, especially when he remembered how guarded she'd been. "It's incredible how God uses our mistakes to set us on the right path. He used my broken relationships to show me how empty and doomed they were without Him at the centre." He swallowed hard. "That's why I've waited years to date anyone again. I needed to wait for the right person to come along."

She blinked. Then toyed with her fingers. Stared at them as if surprised something was missing. Her tan lines showed she'd worn chunky rings. "I know what you mean about empty relationships. I had more than a few during my time of searching."

He was sure she had, but it didn't matter. Her heart belonged to the Lord now. She was on a different path. God's path, as was he. She might be a babe in her faith, but her commitment and hunger to grow was unquestionable.

Could she be the one? *Lord?*

His mother and sister thought so. They wouldn't jest about such things. But what did God think?

He hesitated before placing his hand over hers on the railing. "My mother and sister were obvious tonight with their matchmaking endeavours, but they know of my desire to wait for a clear signal from the Lord before dating anyone now my life is fully focused on Him." He swallowed hard again. "They believe you might be my perfect match."

His heart pounded as he waited for her reaction.

"That's so humbling," she replied before her gaze dropped to their hands.

Goosebumps rose on his arms as she flipped her palm upward, allowing their fingers to intertwine. They fit perfectly together. She tilted her head, her lips twitching into a shy smile. "And do you?"

Goodness. Her boldness surprised him. He cleared his throat. What should he say? "I–I feel deeply honoured that the Lord saw fit to place you in my life." He stared into her gorgeous eyes. "I value my sister's and mother's opinions, and I—I feel the same, Amelia. You're special."

More than special, but that's all he could say for now.

Her eyes glistened.

"I'm sorry. I didn't mean to make you cry. That wasn't my inten—"

Her tearful laugh interrupted him. "It's okay. They're happy tears."

He searched her eyes. "Really?"

She nodded. "Yes."

He was unable to tear his gaze from her as one thought filled him. Consumed him. Thrilled him. The woman standing before him was the one he'd been waiting for. The one God had brought into his life for him to share it with.

He lifted a finger and touched her cheek.

But then he withdrew it. "I'm sorry. I shouldn't have done that."

"It's okay. Don't apologise."

Tenderness softened her gaze, and her mobile lips called to him. He was so tempted to lean down and kiss them, but he needed to be sure. He needed to pray. To get confirmation from God before moving forward. He would never forgive himself if he hurt her.

She turned back to the view but didn't step away from him. He slipped his arm across her shoulders, and she snuggled closer. She fit perfectly—as if they were meant for each other.

Chapter Nine

Amelia's stomach flummoxed. Had Lucas meant what he'd said? She was special? The tender way he'd looked at her, the sheltered way he'd held her, and the gentle way he'd rubbed her forearm... Was it possible he *liked* her? Or had she allowed herself to be swept up in the moment on the porch and read too much into it? Dare she dream they could have a future together? Could this be the path the Lord had for her?

"You're in for a real treat," Willow announced, oblivious of Amelia's inner turmoil as she placed a plate of macadamia nut cookies on the coffee table next to two glasses of cold milk.

Following the game night, they were both clad in pyjamas and socks, and the movie *The Philadelphia Story* was ready on the DVD player. Delicious as the cookies looked, Amelia couldn't muster an appetite. She took one out of politeness as she curled up on the couch. "They look amazing. Thanks."

Willow plopped down beside her and put her feet on the footstool. "Nervous about tomorrow?"

There was that, too. Her first day of worship leading. With Lucas. Her pulse skittered just thinking about him. "I know it's not about me, but I've not led worship before—I don't want to mess it up."

Willow squeezed her shoulder. "From what Lucas tells me, you have nothing to worry about. He said you were great at the audition."

She and Lucas *had* sung well together, and the practice with the other musicians had also gone well. But it wasn't just the singing. It was being with *him*. How could she focus on God with Lucas beside her?

The pink wall clock ticked annoyingly as she stared at the cookie until she felt Willow's gaze boring into her.

Uh-oh. Willow was studying her while hugging a cushion to her chest, her chin resting on top. "What does that face mean?"

Amelia shrugged. "Nothing."

"Hmm… I'm not so sure." She raised one brow suspiciously. "Remember on building day when I told you I thought my brother might like you? I'm starting to think you like him, too. Tell me I'm wrong."

Amelia's jaw dropped. "Y–you're wrong."

Willow lifted her brow further. She wasn't buying it.

With a huff, Amelia dropped her head back against the velvet couch and exhaled. Little point denying it. "Okay, maybe I do like him a little."

Squealing, Willow leaned towards her. "I knew it! You two would make such a great couple!"

Lucas was an amazing man, but was pursuing a relationship so soon after arriving in a new town and changing her lifestyle wise? The Lord had provided her with a great job around great folks, a fabulous place to live, fantastic new friends, and exciting opportunities both alongside Dr. Turner and on the worship team, but expecting to enjoy a potentially lasting relationship with a man like Lucas was too much, too fast. Wasn't it?

"I can't believe you're hesitating." Willow guffawed. "Do you have any idea how many girls have their eyes on him?"

Amelia couldn't help smiling. "I'm not surprised."

He *was* totally cool. She couldn't deny that. Her heart had never beat as fast for anyone before.

All teasing faded from Willow's face. "Many women would love to get Lucas's attention. They're all wonderful ladies, but I've never felt any of them were the right fit."

Amelia's palms began to sweat. She bit into her cookie to distract herself. Buy her time.

"But then I saw him with *you*." Willow waved a hand. "His face lights up when you're around."

Amelia lowered her gaze, although her pulse skittered again, and cookie crumbs stuck in her throat. Could it be possible? Could he like *her*?

But surely he could find someone better than her. More suitable. Without a sordid past. She set the remainder of her cookie aside and hugged her knees to her chest. "We talked about forgiveness during my tryout. He said that Christ's washing away of our sins is total and complete—no additions needed."

"My brother's right." Willow sounded so sure.

The plate of cookies blurred in Amelia's vision. "I know I'm forgiven, but I'm not sure why it's so difficult for me to accept the blessings that have come my way. I can't seem to get over that hurdle of feeling that they're too generous, that I'm unworthy."

Willow scooted closer. "The Bible tells us that the Lord is a Father who loves to give His children good gifts. That you believe the blessings He's sent your way are above what you deserve is awesome and humbling. Don't be afraid to accept them. God's in the business of exceeding our expectations."

Unbidden tears burned her eyes. His love was beyond amazing. Blinking, she rested her chin on her knees. "I don't think I'll ever understand why He's blessed me so much."

"Good. That kind of attitude will ensure you always remain humble and in awe of Him."

They shared a hug before Amelia pulled back. "Well, now we have that settled, should we start the movie?"

Willow shot to her feet. "We have to do one more thing first."

"What's that?"

"Select your outfit for tomorrow!"

"Are you serious?"

"Absolutely."

Amelia frowned. Did it matter what she wore? "We're going to church to glorify the Lord. He doesn't care what I'm wearing."

"Yes, but no harm in sprucing up a little for a certain brother of mine who *might* care...."

Amelia rolled her eyes. "What *am* I going to do with you?"

"There's nothing you can do. You're stuck with me. Like it or lump it." Without another word, Willow reached out and grabbed her by the arm and dragged her towards their bedrooms.

Chapter Ten

It had been years since Lucas had been nervous before a church service. Stepping onto the stage to lead the congregation in worship was as familiar as breathing. But perhaps nervous wasn't the right word to describe these sweeping emotions. It was more a sense of anticipation. A tingling inside. An expectation that the Lord had something incredible in store for Amelia's first day and an eagerness to watch it unfold.

His gaze swept the backstage area once more before he dropped into a chair, allowing the gentle hum of the gathering congregation to settle over his soul. He loved these moments of quiet before the service. To bring glory to God and not himself while leading worship, his heart needed to be in the right place. He exhaled and centred himself.

Lord, guide every word I sing and every note I play this morning and use it for Your Glory. Thank You for bringing Amelia to Water's Edge. I know she's going to be a blessing to the congregation and be greatly used by You. Be with her this morning and fill her with Your peace. He paused. Gulped. *You already know how I feel about her. If it's Your will for us to know each other better, please reveal that to me. I only want to do what's pleasing to You.*

Staring at the floor, he did his best to sort out his thoughts. The vulnerability Amelia had demonstrated in speaking about her past had touched him. He'd never encountered a more sincere admission of the human imperfection shared by all. Her willingness to acknowledge her need for the Lord's merciful cleansing further drew him to her.

Trying to convince himself that the prospect of falling for her didn't frighten him was useless. He'd avoided being in a relationship since coming back to the Lord and rediscovering his purpose. He'd wanted to be sure he was on the right path and fruitful in the areas entrusted to him before becoming involved with anyone. Turning away from God's will led to all sorts of trouble—he'd learned that the hard way. That made him more determined to place every aspect of his life, big or small, in his Father's capable hands.

He wanted nothing more than to receive confirmation that moving forward with Amelia was what God wanted. He was more smitten with her than he'd been with anyone in his life, even Carolyn. But he needed confirmation. From her and from God. Although she'd given small indications, like not pushing him away last night on the porch, he sensed her hesitancy. He didn't blame her. She'd been hurt before. Badly, it seemed.

He wouldn't push her. She'd need to give some signal she was ready and at peace with being more than friends before he acted on his growing affection, but the assurance that *he* might be ready settled inside him, making him open to—and even hopeful for—whatever doors the Father might open.

Footsteps coming down the hall drew him from his musings and to his feet. His heart tumbled in his chest. It was her, in a burnt-orange blouse that highlighted her brown hair and eyes. She'd matched the shirt with a pair of nice jeans and orange flats. Small gold hoops hung from her ears. The tasteful outfit suited her perfectly. And made his heart flutter.

"There she is," he greeted, trying not to sound like a starstruck teenager.

She grinned. "Here I am."

How hard it was not to stare. He cleared his throat. "You look really nice."

Wait a minute. He frowned. Angled his head. Something was different.

Her cheeks grew pink. "Thank you. I–I let Willow do my makeup."

"Ah! That's it. Don't get me wrong—you look great without it. But Willow did a good job." He rolled his eyes towards the ceiling. What a goofball. "This compliment's not coming out the way I'd hoped."

Her soft laughter rushed around him. "It's all right. Thanks for saying it. I haven't worn much makeup since arriving here."

His brow quirked. "You used to wear it?"

"In the places I worked, they wanted us girls to look a certain way... like pin-up girls. 'Cover your blemishes. Make yourself look as attractive as possible to get better tips.' So, I'd layer on makeup to disguise my imperfections."

He folded his arms and studied her. "I fail to see any. Care to point them out?"

She waved her hands in front of her face. "Oh... my skin is kind of ruddy, so I always tried to smooth out the tone. And more mascara and the right eyeliner application made my eyes look bigger. Things like that."

Poor girl. She'd allowed insignificant details to dictate how she saw herself. The features she'd brought up never crossed his mind. When he looked into her eyes, he saw only the sweet, sensitive, and kind woman he'd come to admire.

He hesitated before stepping towards her. "Well, I'll tell you now that covering up your imperfections is nonsense. I'm sure there's no room for nonsense in your life. Am I right?"

She fiddled with her hair, tucking strands behind her ears as she ducked her head. "Since I left the bar, I've avoided wearing it. I didn't feel the need to, but today, Willow showed me how to apply just a little." Another blush crept into her cheeks. "I hope it looks all right."

As much as he wanted to tell her she'd look beautiful no matter what she put on her face, he kept that thought to himself. "Well, you look really nice." He cleared his throat again and reached for his guitar. It was time to slow his beating heart and get his mind on the service. "Ready?"

"I'm not sure." She let out a heavy breath. "I feel crazy nervous."

"You'll be fine. I know you will be, but let's pray about it, shall we?"

The sudden light in her eyes did strange things to his insides. "Sure. I'd like that."

He stepped closer and placed his hand on her shoulder. "Dear Lord and heavenly Father, please still Amelia's nerves. May her heart be focused on You as she helps lead worship this morning. Reach deep inside her and give her peace and assurance of Your abiding love and care for her. In Jesus' precious name. Amen."

When she opened her eyes, they glistened. "Thank you."

"You're more than welcome. After you." He motioned for her to go ahead. The other worship leaders—Adam, who played the drums, and Sally, a young mum who played the keyboard—stood at the sanctuary's side entrance.

Giving a nod, he sent another silent prayer upwards while they made their way onto the stage.

As he settled in front of the congregation, warmth flooded him. Leading these people in worship was such a privilege. When he glanced at Amelia, her gaze was on him. One nod of his head and he and the other musicians began playing, filling the sanctuary with God-honouring music. Once Amelia's voice entered the mix, his heart soared. There was no need to look around to know one thing for certain: *she* was the Lord's instrument.

It wasn't until the final song of their opening line-up that he looked at her again. Her face glowed as she held the microphone. The Lord had not only touched the congregation with her voice, but *her*. A knot formed in his throat. Thankfully, the final song was coming to an end, and Pastor Noah strode onto the stage. The worship team filed down the steps and joined their friends and family in the pews. Willow beamed as Amelia joined her. He sent his sister a smile before he settled down in the front row next to Adam. As much as he would have liked to join Amelia and Willow, he needed to collect his thoughts.

The God-breathed message Pastor Noah brought to the congregation fed his soul, and by the time the closing prayer was given, Lucas felt at rest about the subject he'd prayed about only an hour earlier: *Amelia*.

The worship team led the church in a final hymn before folks broke off into groups to fellowship amongst themselves. When Amelia sought him out, she was still glowing. "That was the most wonderful experience of my life," she gushed. "I'm so grateful for the opportunity. For all of it, actually!"

"It *was* a beautiful service, and you did so well. I'm already looking forward to next week."

Her face brightened even further. "So am I. I'll see you on Friday night for practice?"

His heart pounded. His hands grew clammy. His words came out in a rush. "I was hoping I might see you before then."

Her forehead scrunched. "Oh, you think we should add an additional session? Sure, I can do anytime—"

"No," he interjected before he lost his nerve. "I was hoping you'd agree to a date."

Her eyes shot open.

Had he made a mistake? Got it all wrong?

But, when her expression turned from shock to excitement, relief filled him. He hadn't been as far off base as he'd feared.

"I'd love to." Her eyes shone. "Wh—what did you have in mind?"

Suddenly mischievous, he narrowed his eyes. "I'm not going to tell you. It's a surprise."

She laughed and raised her hands. "All right, but do I get to know what day and time so I'm ready?"

"Let's do Tuesday. I'll pick you up at six p.m. Sharp," he added, continuing the light teasing vein they'd entered.

"Sharp," she repeated with a wink. "Sounds good. I'll see you then."

As she rejoined Willow, her grin told him there was no need to tell her to be on time. She was as ready for this date as he was. But Tuesday was an eternity away.

The following day, Amelia rapped on Dr. Turner's door, balancing a box of supplies in the crook of one arm. "Dr. Turner?"

"Come in," his friendly voice replied.

Pushing the door open, she made her way inside. "I brought some donations that were left at the diner." She set the box on the edge of his desk. "Charlotte said they're from a Mrs. Warren. She asked if we could drop them to you as she was in a hurry."

"Ah, yes." Dr. Turner stood. "She owns the adult foster home here and faithfully passes any leftover supplies she acquires to me." He sifted through the box's contents. "It's so nice that folks look out for each other. It's something I'll never take for granted about Water's Edge."

He had no idea just how amazing she found that.

"I wanted to thank you again for your help on the first building day," he went on.

She clasped her hands behind her back. "I enjoyed it."

He looked up from the box, his expression thoughtful. "Was Willow right when she mentioned you were interested in nursing?"

She shrugged, her hands tightening their grip behind her.

"It's more like a pipe dream. The opportunity to attend school never lined up for me."

"Been working since you were young, haven't you?"

Her head cocked to one side. "How did you guess?"

He sat at his desk and motioned for her to pull up a chair. Once she'd done so, he continued. "I was much like you as a young man. My family life, my financial situation... Nothing made it easy for me to pursue higher education. But I knew I was meant to be a doctor."

Her eyes narrowed. "How did you know?"

Fingers drumming on the armrests, he leaned back in his chair. "I'll be honest with you. I wasn't very good in school. That is, until I took my first anatomy class in high school. The way cars and trucks set the imagination of some on fire, that's what science did for me."

She could just see him. "So, you found what you were good at."

He rocked back further and raised one hand. "It was more than that. For once, an academic subject clicked for me, yes. But the approach my teacher took clued me into my purpose."

She leaned in. This was getting interesting.

"My teacher was a retired doctor who rejoined the workforce because of his passion for anatomy and his desire to pour that into young lives. Praise God, he decided to come back. If it wasn't for his class and his passion for teaching not only about the human body but also the importance of compassion in medicine, I doubt I'd have recognised my calling. After a year in his class, I knew. Ring any bells?"

She exhaled. "I never put much store in 'callings.' To be honest, until I came to Christ, I didn't believe we were placed on earth for a reason. But I have to admit, when I worked at the assisted living facility, I felt the most fulfilled, like I had a purpose. Helping ease the pain of others and making the lives of the elderly a little easier did something inside of me that working in a bar never did."

"You might not have known the Creator then, but it sounds like you were on to something."

Good point. Why'd she leave? Things could have been so different if she hadn't drifted into bar work. "Exactly. And now I know that people have souls and a reason for being on this earth. In a way, it makes helping them through the pain of this life seem more meaningful, doesn't it?"

"It does." He ran a hand along his jaw. "You know, Amelia, there's no reason you can't pursue your passion for medicine now. I'd be glad to help you."

Her eyes widened, and her heart quickened. Had she heard correctly? This kind doctor was offering to help *her?*

His bushy brows rose. "But no pressure. It's simply an offer."

Snapping out of her daze, she shook her head so hard her hair slapped her cheeks. "It's not that. I just..." She sat back, laughing. "It feels too good to be true."

"It's not." He laid one hand over hers. "I need an assistant, and you've had some experience. If you'd like to work with me, I can provide you with a letter of recommendation, and we can see about nursing school options."

Her mind whirled. Since her arrival in town, the Lord had handed her unexpected blessings, and now Dr. Turner was handing her the keys to a new world of possibilities—a potential entrance to a door she'd been certain was shut to her. "I don't know what to say."

"No need to say anything right now. Go ahead and give it some thought and prayer, and then let me know. My offer isn't going anywhere."

Still processing the enormity of this opportunity, she hesitated. "Don't you want to do a formal interview? Maybe I should bring you a resume?"

His head shaking, he squeezed her hand. "Your day as my first aid helper and this talk are more than enough of an interview. Take your time deciding. If you feel led, reach out. You know where to find me."

Despite the unexpected nature of this proposal, everything within her desired to say yes. However, he was right about giving it thought and prayer. This was indeed an important decision. She *would* think and pray on it, but she'd be back in this office soon—hopefully with a positive response.

Chapter Eleven

Early on Tuesday evening, Amelia once again found herself at the mercy of Willow's fashion assistance. She didn't mind. Being so nervous about her date, she doubted she'd put together a proper outfit if left to her own devices. While her mind was all over the place, her roommate mixed and matched shirts with pants and skirts with tops in search of what she considered the perfect first-date combination.

"I've got it!" Willow brandished a modest cream-coloured top featuring delicate lace detail along the neckline and sleeves. She'd chosen Amelia's nicest pair of jeans and a pair of pumps.

Amelia managed a smile. "That's the one, huh? You're sure it's not too casual?"

Willow laughed. "My incorrigible brother refused to tell you where you're going, making it kinda hard to know for certain. So, under the circumstances, yes, I feel this outfit is perfect." Grinning, she rolled her eyes upwards. "It *is* kind of romantic that he wants it to be a surprise. I can't wait to hear where he takes you."

The butterflies dancing in Amelia's stomach fluttered faster, beating against her insides as if begging release. "I'm wondering too."

Willow pressed the outfit into her arms, shooing her with her hands. "You'll never find out if you don't get ready. Go get dressed and come back so we can work on your hair."

Amelia did as she was bade. When she returned, Willow held a hairbrush, ready to attack.

"I was thinking my hair should be up." Amelia settled on a chair in front of the dresser.

Willow vetoed with a headshake. "No way these gorgeous locks are going up. Not tonight." She took a step back, her brow lowering as she studied the back of Amelia's head. After a moment, she grabbed a few bobby pins and got to work.

In record time, Willow had pulled back the hair on both sides of Amelia's face, creating attractive twists that showed off her silver earrings and allowed the rest of her hair to cascade down her back. "Perfect," she said. "Now, for your makeup."

Grateful for the excuse to close her eyes, Amelia allowed her roommate to have her way with the mascara and eyeshadow and took the opportunity to pray once again. She did feel peace about getting to know Lucas as more than a friend, but anxiety was doing its best to wrap itself around her heart. What if she made a mess of things? If they ran out of topics to talk about? If he wanted more than she could offer? What *did* she have to offer, really? She was a barmaid who now worked in a diner, although Dr. Turner's offer could change that. The only thing she had going for her right now was her new status as a child of God. Would that be enough for Lucas?

Lord, I commit this night to You. Calm my nerves. You know how anxious I am. I don't want to make a mess of it.

By the time Willow ordered her to open her eyes, the tension in Amelia's neck had eased and calm had settled over her.

Willow swept a hand towards the mirror. "What do you think?"

Wow. Amelia stifled a gasp and scooted closer to the glass. How did she do it? Willow's makeup choice was perfect. Not too much, not too little.

"Amelia! You look great."

They both turned at the unexpected voice. Sheila stood in the doorway, beaming.

Amelia grinned. "It's all thanks to your daughter."

Sheila stepped forward, her eyes aglow, her hands extended. "No matter how skilled Willow is, your natural beauty shines through, Amelia."

"She's right." Willow nodded.

Natural beauty? What were they talking about? Her skin was ruddy, her nose big, her eyes small. She'd gotten her father's genes, not her mother's. Pity, because her mother had been a looker.

"I'm not so sure about that."

Sheila rested her hands on Amelia's shoulders. "'Your beauty should not come from outward adornment, such as elaborate hairstyles and the wearing of gold jewellery or fine clothes. Rather, it should be that of your inner self, the unfading beauty of a gentle and quiet spirit, which is of great worth in God's sight'—First Peter three, verses three and four."

She knew those verses word for word? Amelia blinked.

"It's what's inside that's important," Shelia continued. "You look gorgeous. I think Lucas will be gobsmacked, but it's your inner beauty that truly shines."

Amelia blinked again, this time shooing away tears. This woman, this godly woman, thought she had inner beauty? Had God changed her so much? Because the old Amelia Anderson didn't possess that kind of beauty.

"I–I can't thank you both enough for all you've done for me. Both of you." Her gaze swung to Willow and then back to Sheila.

Sheila's eyes grew moist. "You don't understand what a blessing you are to *us*, do you?"

Amelia angled her head. How could she be a blessing to these two women? "I–I don't understand."

Willow threw an arm across her shoulders, laughing. "Of course, you don't. You're not the one who's been waiting around for years for Lucas to find the right woman."

Ducking her head, Amelia fiddled with the new cross necklace Willow had given her. "You think I'm the right one for him? We haven't even gone on a date yet."

Sheila rubbed her arm. "I'm his mother. Mothers have a sense about these things."

Willow chuckled. "This mother, more than any other, in my opinion."

Amelia could only stare. The love these women held for Lucas was undeniable. For that reason, being viewed as a match for him was the highest compliment she could imagine. When she managed to respond, emotion whispered through her voice. "That means so much to me."

Sheila sniffed. "I knew God would orchestrate everything for the good when it came to my son. I was prepared to wait as long as the good Lord deemed necessary. But now, here you are."

Willow tucked a strand of hair behind Amelia's ear and kissed her cheek, and her tenderness brought fresh tears to Amelia's eyes.

"Stop it, you two!" she protested, fanning her eyes with both hands. "You're going to ruin my makeup."

"We can't have that." Sheila chuckled as she dabbed her own eyes.

A car pulling into the driveway saved Amelia from further embarrassment.

"There he is." Willow pulled the curtain back and glanced out the window. "We need to pull ourselves together." After also drying her eyes, she fluffed Amelia's hair. "You look gorgeous."

Amelia made a move towards the door.

"Stop!" Willow's horrified gasp forbade her from taking another step. "A woman should always let the man come to the door and knock."

Oh. There were dating rules. This was already so different to anything Amelia'd ever experienced. She'd been with guys before, but never on a proper date. She was going to make a mess of it. She just knew it. Her hands grew clammy. *Lord, please calm my heart.*

The knock came. Her pulse raced.

"Off you go." Willow nodded towards the door, her eyes sparkling. "But give me a hug first."

After she pulled Amelia in for a quick embrace, Sheila did the same.

Okay. Enough.

Gulping, Amelia left the two women and headed out the bedroom door and walked down the short blue hallway before pausing at the front door. She ran her hands down her top, adjusted it, and then took a deep breath before turning the knob.

Lucas stood on the porch, a bunch of flowers in his hand—his hair immaculately combed, his face clean-shaven, his woodsy cologne intriguing. The blue of his freshly pressed collared shirt brought out the brilliance of his eyes, making them more alluring.

Her heart beat double time. This *was* happening.

Smiling, he stepped forward and held out the flowers. "For my beautiful date."

Goodness. No one had brought her flowers before. She accepted the bright blooms and thanked him.

"My pleasure. You look amazing, by the way." The adoration in his eyes was by far the tenderest thing she'd ever seen.

"Thank you." Her voice almost caught.

Willow stood behind her, craning her neck over Amelia's shoulder. "Off you two go. Have a great time."

Over her shoulder, Amelia caught Willow's gaze as Willow snagged the bouquet and Lucas placed his hand lightly on the small of Amelia's back.

Willow gave a single nod, and both she and her mother waved while Lucas guided Amelia down the three steps.

It was a relief to sit in the car—even if it smelled like his woodsy aftershave, making her hyperaware of him. Expelling a breath, she faced him when he slid into the driver's seat. "Now are you going to tell me where we're going?"

His mouth tipped in a lopsided grin as he turned on the ignition and reversed down the driveway. "You thought I was going to give in that easily?"

She laughed. "Not really, but it was worth a try, right?"

"I *will* tell you the place we're stopping at before heading to our actual destination is one you know well."

She scrunched her brows. "Let me guess. The diner?"

His eyes widened. "How did you know?"

She shrugged. "I'm just smart, I suppose."

"Yeah, you are." His smile sent a tingle up her spine. But then his voice grew serious while he headed his fancy sports car down the road. "I hear you're going to be Dr. Turner's assistant."

Wow. News sure did travel fast in this town. She'd only told Willow that Dr. Turner had offered her a job. And she was still praying about it. Although there was little to pray about. It was a no-brainer. She wasn't sure why she hadn't already accepted the offer.

"I'm–I'm still praying about it."

"I can't see why God would say no, so I'm excited for you. And proud of you. You'll make a wonderful assistant."

Warmth surged through her. Although she'd have to speak with Willow. Why would she have shared such information with her brother? Did the whole town know?

"Thank you. And yes, I think I'll take it."

Her gaze remained on her hands, clasped firmly in her lap and looking so different without the heavy rings, before she glanced out the corner of her eye. Her heart skipped a beat when their gazes met.

Moments passed before he turned right and drove past the Greek homes. "Did I tell you how beautiful you look?"

Her chest warmed. "You said something to that effect back at the house, but I don't mind you saying it again." Her pulse accelerated when he reached his hand out and placed it over hers.

"I'll have you know I'm going to take that as an invitation to remind you of it whenever I want to."

She studied his profile. He was such a handsome man. She could so easily fall in love with him. Anticipation tingled through her as she turned her attention back to the road before them. They wove up a steep hill, more whitewashed homes with blue shutters on each side. Amelia could almost imagine they were in Greece.

At the diner, Charlotte was waiting outside, holding a box. She hurried to the driver's side window before Lucas had a chance to kill the engine.

Amelia frowned. What was going on?

"I kept everything under the heat lamp until I saw you coming," Charlotte explained, her face shining.

Lucas accepted the boxed food and placed it on the back seat. "Thanks for preparing this, Charlotte. It smells great."

She waved his words off and grinned at Amelia. "It's my pleasure. You two have a good time, now."

Seemed the whole town knew about their date.

The mouth-watering aroma of Charlotte's famous chicken and mushroom risotto overpowered Lucas's aftershave as he pulled back onto the road.

Amelia twisted to face him when they arrived at the Youth Centre. Was this his surprise? "What are we doing here? Did you finish the building?"

He shook his head and reached for the food. "Not yet. But, finished or not, the building site is still home to the best starlit view in town. After my parents' place, of course."

Barely containing her excitement, she wiggled in her seat as she waited for him to come around to the passenger's side to open her car door. Warmth spread up her arm when she took the hand he offered.

They made their way towards the partly built centre. A good deal of work had been done since that first day. The framing was complete, the roof on.

"It's looking great," she said.

Gratitude shone in his eyes as he surveyed the structure. "It's coming along nicely."

"That's no surprise." She felt at ease enough to allow her teasing spirit to come out. If he could be lighthearted and jovial, so could she. She winked at him. "They have a good architect overseeing the project."

His mouth went slack, but then he gave a mock bow. "Well, thank you."

Hand-in-hand, they walked along as the colours of the sunset deepened. Watching the sky's slow, steady progress as it turned into a radiant painting reminded her of the way the Lord had been working in her life. God was faithfully moving, sometimes behind the scenes, like with Lucas. She didn't notice He'd been laying the groundwork until the blessing was revealed, like the fantastic streaks of colour that appeared almost out of nowhere.

"Watch your step," Lucas said at the foot of the ladder leading to the second storey.

She raised a brow. "Are you sure this is a good idea? Do I have to remind you what happened the last time I climbed a ladder?"

The brush of his breath against her ear as he leaned in caused goosebumps on her arms. "No, you don't have to remind me. But today, I'm right here to catch you should the need arise. I've got you."

Her heart fluttering, she stepped onto the first rung and took extra care with the foot she injured, though Lucas's close presence behind reassured her.

Any inhibitions she'd harboured about the climb vanished when she sighted the view. It truly was the most beautiful vantage point in Water's Edge, rivalling his parents' front porch.

"It's gorgeous." So taken with the view, she tripped on the edge of the ladder.

"Easy, there." Grinning, he grabbed her arm just before she toppled.

She caught her breath, her hand going to his chest to steady herself. She could feel his heart pounding beneath her palm.

Did he know hers was hammering as well?

"Told you I'd catch you." Though his tone was teasing, there was no missing the intensity in his blue eyes.

It was impossible to look away. Her lungs seemed to stop. Was he about to kiss her? She swallowed hard as he lowered his mouth and brushed his lips against hers with the utmost tenderness. Though the gesture was soft, the kiss lingered for many moments, leaving her breathless.

His heart was in his eyes as he placed the food box on the

floor and took her in his arms. "Thank you for coming here with me this evening," he whispered into her hair. "You seem too good to be true at times."

A laugh issued from her lips as she breathed in his cologne's woodsy scent. "You took the words right out of my mouth."

He gave her a gentle squeeze. "Shall we take a seat and bask in amazement together?"

She was all for that. Amazement at Lucas. Amazement at God. Amazement at Him seeing fit to turn everything that had happened to her thus far into something beautiful.

Lucas kept hold of her hand as he led her along the flat roof. They settled down, allowing their legs to dangle off the edge, giving them a flawless view of the starry expanse and shimmery sea.

The light salty breeze ruffled her hair and tickled her nose. "This has to be the best place in all of Water's Edge." Sighing, she scooted closer and rested her head on his shoulder.

He slipped an arm around her and rubbed her forearm, pulling her closer. "I agree. And I've been hoping you'll want to have some role here once the centre's operational."

She blinked. A role? What kind of role?

He continued. "You were so great with the kids in the children's wing that I thought you might enjoy being a part of things once we get going."

She was such a babe in the faith. How could he even think she could work with youth? Leading worship was one thing, but leading young people was totally different. "I don't think I'm qualified for that. I don't have all the answers."

She was still figuring things out for herself. How could he suggest she help guide young minds?

"No one expects you to. But that's not a problem. No one does."

He ran his hand up and down her arm. "I've thought a great deal about what you said the day of your singing audition about not feeling worthy." He looked down at her. "Telling you to not feel unworthy doesn't solve anything, does it?"

"I guess not." It was true. How many times had he and Willow already told her that, and yet she couldn't shake that feeling of being of lesser value in God's eyes than other Christians.

"Will you allow me to tell you what I see when I look at you?"

Tipping her head, she faced him. As his genuine affection wiped away any fears over the prospect of his honest opinion, she nodded.

His eyes searched her face, his gaze moving from her forehead to her eyes to her nose and mouth. "When I heard you singing to comfort Ezekiel, I was awestruck by your vocal abilities. But it wasn't until after your audition when you sang with the worship team that it hit me: you're a tangible representation of Christ's ability to redeem and make whole those who are lost, who feel unworthy—*especially* those who feel unworthy. He's so clearly changed your life, and He's using you for His glory with your singing."

His voice faltered.

"Lucas...?"

He looked straight at her, holding her gaze even as his eyes moistened. He lifted two fingers and ran them down her cheek. "You've reminded me once again of His goodness, Amelia. All the time I spent running wasn't in vain. He used it. He's using us both—no matter what our pasts have been. None of us will ever be perfect teachers or Christians or human beings, but He uses us regardless. He wants us to be available and obedient and to represent Him."

He was right. There was no need for her to know everything. God could use her as long as her heart was open to His leading. She reached up and brushed a tear from Lucas's cheek. "Thank you. That helps a lot."

He laid his hand on top of hers, pressing her palm to his cheek. "We helped each other. You helped me remember what redemption looks like. That's part of the reason why you'd be an asset here at the centre. The concept that God's love covers us all, no matter what, needs to be at the forefront of our mission. Kids need to know they're loved, no matter what they've done. No one can portray that better than those who've experienced brokenness and whom God is transforming by His love."

She tucked her cheek into his palm, fitting to the curve of his hand, warming at his touch and his touching words. "You're saying I'm the worst of sinners?"

"No, but maybe close to it."

Laughing with him, she fell into his arms.

He kissed the top of her head. "So, what do you say? Would you like to be involved?"

She drew a slow breath. "Can I pray about it?"

"Absolutely."

He pulled back and looked at her, his expression sobering. "I know we haven't eaten yet. But I want to ask you something, and I don't think I can wait."

Her forehead scrunched. "Yes...?"

Gathering her hands into his, he cradled them beneath his chin. "We've only known each other a short time, but I believe God orchestrates everything according to His perfect plan. And I can see now that He planned for us to meet at this exact time in both of our journeys. I also believe He was preparing our hearts so, when we met, we'd be ready."

Goodness. Was he going to propose? Her pulse quickened. She wasn't ready for that. No way.

She gulped.

"You're the most gorgeous woman I've ever met, inside and out. My heart beats faster when I'm with you. You do strange things to my insides. I hope you feel the same about me. I think you do."

No way could she respond, but somehow, she managed a slow nod.

He smiled. "That's great. Okay, this can't wait any longer."

As her shoulders inched up by her ears, she barely stifled a gasp.

"Amelia, would you do me the honour of allowing me to officially court you?"

Court her? How old-fashioned was that? The tension drained from her shoulders. At least he hadn't proposed.

He continued. "I've been praying about this, and I was committed to waiting until I was sure it was the right time. I wanted to know I had the Lord's blessing, and now I feel He's given me that reassurance over and over again as I've watched you and talked to you."

"There's no need to convince me, Lucas. I've discussed this with the Lord, too."

"And?"

"And it's a yes. I'd love to be courted by you. I can't think of anything I'd love more."

His eyes lit, and a mischievous glint twinkled in their blue. "Except perhaps what comes after the courting phase."

Her eyes widened. Marriage? He'd already made the leap to imagining a life with her? Oh goodness. This was too much.

"I can't wait to begin this journey with you, Amelia." He traced a finger down her hairline. "God has been so good to us."

Her heart hammered as he lowered his mouth. The first touch of his lips against hers made her gasp. He kissed her slowly, tenderly. It was unlike any kiss she'd had before. Closing her eyes, she responded in kind.

God indeed had been good.

Chapter Twelve

"Not too shabby, boss." Lucas straightened to his full height, bending backwards to stretch his lower back. "It's coming along."

"It's more than coming along." Adam motioned to the Youth Centre's recreation room in its entirety. "You've almost single-handedly finished the flooring in one afternoon. I'm impressed."

Lucas took a long drink from a plastic water bottle before wiping the sweat from his brow with his handkerchief. "I guess I'm on a roll."

His expression knowing, Adam crossed his arms over his chest and leaned one shoulder against the unpainted wall. "It's more than that. You have renewed energy."

Lucas tucked the handkerchief back into his pocket as he surveyed the floorboards yet to be laid. "Is that so?"

"Yes, and I know the source." Adam's brows rose when

Lucas offered no response. "When were you planning on letting us all in on the news?"

Lucas chuckled. "What did you want me to do? Make an announcement before Pastor Noah's sermon on Sunday?"

"You know what I mean." Adam waved off his sarcasm. "We've all been waiting for you and Amelia to make things official."

That was news to Lucas and amused him no end. "So, Willow and my mum weren't the only ones getting ideas about our futures, huh?"

Completely serious, Adam shook his head. "She hasn't been in Water's Edge for long, but we all saw it right away. Congratulations, brother."

Lucas clapped him on the shoulder. "Thanks, mate. We're excited about what the future holds for us."

"She's a keeper."

"She sure is. I never thought I could be so inspired by anyone, but the way she's taken to life here in Water's Edge and how her love for the Lord and for the people here has grown so much has been nothing short of amazing."

"God made everything fall into line just right, didn't He?"

Lucas nodded. "No question about it."

Adam glanced at his watch. "I left the materials you ordered in the front room. I need to head to Dr. Turner's and get the assignment schedule for the next community building day. I'll catch up with you soon."

"Sounds good. Catch you."

Adam's words lingered long after he left the centre and Lucas returned to laying floorboards. God *had* made everything fall into place at the right time. The way He'd worked was mind-blowing and humbling.

Lord, thank You for Your abundant blessings. Thank You for bringing Amelia into my life. Bless our relationship. May we together bring glory and honour to You in all we do, think, and say.

※

Having been on her own from a young age, Amelia was used to working hard. Many times over the years she'd been so tired she'd fallen asleep in her clothes when she got home in the wee hours of the morning after a long shift. Today, as she dressed for work, she was tired, but it was a different kind of tired. A good kind. Between working at the diner and with Dr. Turner and helping with the Youth Centre, her days brimmed with activity, wearing her out. The thrill of her budding relationship with Lucas only added to the blissful whirlwind. Sheila often told her to slow down, that there was no need to spread herself thin, to which Amelia assured her she felt anything but spread thin. This new reality that seemed too good to be true was better than anything she'd ever experienced. She didn't want to miss a single thing.

On Friday morning two weeks after their memorable Youth Centre first date, she gathered her apron and work shoes, poured herself a mug of coffee, and headed to the door. Charlotte always had an abundance of caffeine at the ready, but Amelia had a late night and wasn't sure she'd make it without coffee for the road. Not that it was a long trip. Nothing was far in Water's Edge.

She smiled, thinking back to the evening she and Lucas

discussed their hopes and dreams for their own lives and for the Youth Centre. They'd stayed on the roof until nearly midnight discussing everything from potential summer activities for the youth to Adam's most recent Bible Study and how fortunate they felt to have found one another. They both agreed taking things slowly would be best, but neither was good at refraining from venturing into everything they hoped to do together. For Amelia, it was beyond anything she could have ever imagined.

She'd just pulled up to the diner when her phone rang. She frowned at the unfamiliar number. A glance at the time assured her she still had fifteen minutes before her shift, so she answered. "Hello?"

"Amelia? Goodness, I hardly recognise your voice."

A lump formed in her throat as she clutched the phone. "Mum?"

The responding laugh on the other end was soft, unlike what Amelia remembered.

"You sound different, too."

"Well, time changes people, doesn't it?" her mother remarked.

The cars parked before the diner blurred, and the squawking of the resident seagulls faded. Her mother hadn't the faintest idea just how true that was. And not such a great deal of time—a few weeks, even. "Yes, it does." She cleared her throat, rubbing the suddenly sweaty palm of her free hand down her skirt. "So, how are you doing? It's been a long time."

The bitter chuckle rasped through the speakers and grated Amelia's nerves. "Four years and three months to be exact."

Dread gathered in her stomach. There was a good reason she and her mother rarely spoke: every conversation turned into an argument. Much of that stemmed from Amelia moving out as soon as she could. Her mother had accused her of running from her problems. Amelia, however, had justified her decision as a necessary escape because the issues at home were messing with her.

Surrounded by her parents' constant strife, she'd scarcely been able to breathe, so she'd gotten out. Escaped.

She'd reached out to her parents only a few times since. Conversations had lasted just long enough for her to learn that her father was in prison for theft and that turning any topic into a fight with her mother was as easy as ever. After that, she hadn't bothered trying to contact them. She'd figured her mother had no problem with this as they'd parted on ill terms. However, her knowing the last time they'd talked, down to the month, implied differently.

"You have a different number," Amelia said as she cast around for something more meaningful to say.

"Yes." A tense silence followed before her mother continued. "Where are you living these days? Still in Sydney? Are you bartending, or have you moved up the ranks to being the entertainment?"

Every fibre of Amelia's being recoiled. Still, she couldn't blame her. With the way she'd moved from bar to bar for work, associating with people whose reputations were far from reputable, the idea that she'd end up in shadier lines of work was not far-fetched.

"No, Mum. I'm in a little town called Water's Edge."

"Water's Edge?" her mother repeated.

Amelia's brow lowered when her mother pulled the phone away to cough. She didn't remember her having a cough.

"What on earth are you doing in a town like that? You must be bored out of your mind."

"Far from it," Amelia answered. "It's a great place to live. I like it a lot. In fact, it's where I want to settle."

"Settle? You?" her mother scoffed. "In yer dreams, luv."

Amelia bristled, but let it go. Usually, her mother's careless remarks hurt. And up until recently, she would have been right. The idea of settling would have been a joke. She'd been searching for fulfillment and meaning but had never found it until she arrived there. And now, the need to wander was gone.

"Things are different here, Mum," she ventured. "*I'm* different."

"Is that so?"

"Yes."

Another brief silence.

"How are things with you, Mum?"

"If you're asking if I'm in good health, I'm not."

Amelia's heart sank. "Oh, I'm sorry to hear that. I heard you coughing—"

"I have cancer, Amelia."

All at once, everything around her—the clock reminding her that she needed to get to her shift, the customers filing into the diner, the seagulls squawking near the bin—came to a standstill. "What? Oh my." The emotions at war within her threatened to take over. "Are you getting the treatment you need?"

"I don't have money, Amelia."

Her mother's sharp tone hurt, but, for the first time, Amelia was able to accept that her words were spoken out of fear and not with the sole intention of angering her.

"I'm getting what the system can provide," she went on. "But at this point, it doesn't seem that even the most advanced treatments could save me."

"It's in your lungs, then?" Amelia whispered, working hard to grasp all this.

"Yes." Mum laughed. "If you're still a smoker, I'd suggest you quit now."

Though she could have assured her mother she'd quit with no desire to go back, Amelia couldn't summon the words.

"I thought of calling you back in the beginning, but I didn't think there'd be any point—after all, you never had time to visit in the past."

Not for the first time during the last weeks, Amelia found herself speaking from her heart before her mind had a chance to say no. "I'm free to come and visit you now."

"Aren't you too busy with whatever kind of work you're doing?"

Things *were* insane, but... "I can make it work. Would this coming week be okay with you?"

"Y–yes..." Her mother stretched out the hesitant word. "Yes, that would be fine."

"Great." The queue of customers at the diner was out the door now, making it impossible to ignore her shift any longer. "I have to go to work now, but I'll be in touch."

Amelia's pulse was pounding by the time they rang off. She grabbed her apron and climbed out of the car, but how could she focus? Her mother had cancer. *Oh Lord, You know my mother and I don't see eye to eye on anything, but I pray for her right now. Let her open her heart to You. Reveal Yourself to her just like You revealed Yourself to me. And, Lord, please heal her from her cancer if it's Your will. And please help me focus on my shift. In Jesus' precious name. Amen.*

※

Stretching his arms over his head, Lucas dialled Amelia's number. His shoulders ached from another day of manual labour, but he couldn't think of a more satisfying feeling. The only thing that would make today better was hearing Amelia's voice. He smiled when she answered.

"Hey, there."

"Hi, Lucas."

His smile faded at her dejected tone. "Is something wrong?"

"I'm okay."

He settled on the edge of his bed, rumpling the grey plaid doona cover, and switched his phone to the other ear. "You don't sound okay." As the silence stretched between them, his stomach tightened. "Amelia?"

When a sob cracked on the other end of the line, his heart fell.

"Oh, Lucas, something's happened."

"What is it?" He clenched the phone, his teeth clenching as well. "You can tell me."

"I know." She sniffed. "But do you mind coming over? I need to see you."

He was already on his feet and reaching for his car keys. "I'll be there in a jiffy."

Though the drive to Willow and Amelia's house took less than ten minutes, it was enough time for his thoughts to fly in all directions. What had caused her to be so upset?

By the time he reached her doorstep, he had no idea what to expect, but when she opened the door, his heart wrung. Though she'd clearly done her best to compose herself, there was no missing the redness around her eyes and the wobble in her smile.

"Thanks for coming."

Unable to resist any longer, he took her in his arms. "Of course. Tell me what's wrong."

She melted against him, allowing him to hold her for many moments before she stepped back. "Come on in."

In the living room, she wrapped her arms around herself, looking small and vulnerable in an oversized T-shirt and baggy track pants.

"Can I get you anything to drink?" she asked.

"No, but thanks. Why don't you come sit down?" He nodded towards the couch.

She sat next to him, her mouth pressed into a fretful line. "I heard from my mum today."

He blinked. Wow. She and her mother were estranged, so that had to have been a shock. "Really? How is she?"

Tears filled Amelia's eyes. "She has cancer."

"Oh, sweetheart..."

She covered her face with her hands.

He embraced her, holding her close as sobs racked her body.

When she found her voice, hiccups riddled her words. "It took me by surprise. I didn't even know how to respond. She sounds so helpless and..."

He brushed a lock of hair from her tear-streaked face. "And what?"

She blinked up at him, took a deep breath. "The malice I

normally feel for her wasn't there. I just felt sorry that she's alone and bitter. She seems so lost." She swiped at her damp cheeks. "When I talked to her before, all I ever thought about was how she was trying to turn everything into an argument. But I can see it clearly now—she's lost, just like I was. She desperately needs God, Lucas."

His hands came up to cup her face, which was becoming dearer to him with each passing day. "And this is the perfect opportunity to tell her about Him."

"You're right." She managed a watery smile. "I can't guarantee seeing her won't bring up feelings from the past, but I've had practice in accepting the forgiveness Jesus offers. Now it's time to share it."

He was so proud of her. "Exactly. You never know how God can use You if you don't try."

She nodded, already looking stronger. "I don't know how long she's got."

"Would you like me to go with you to see her?"

Drawing in another long breath, she glanced at her hands before shaking her head. "Thanks, but I should go alone. But knowing you're here waiting for me will give me the strength I need. With God's help, I can do this."

"I know you can." He lifted her hand to his lips. "For one frightening moment, I was worried you were going to tell me you didn't want to date me."

Wisps of hair stuck to her damp cheeks as she shook her head. "I'd never say that, Lucas." Gripping his hands, she looked deep into his eyes. "I can't tell you how grateful I am to have your support. You have no idea."

He tucked a strand of her loose hair behind her ear. "I'll be here for you no matter what. We're in this together. You, me, and God."

Tears welled in her eyes again. He pulled her close and held her. "Lord, bless Amelia and go with her. Be her strength and her portion. Use her for Your glory. Soften her mother's heart that it might be open to Your healing love. In Jesus' precious name. Amen."

Chapter Thirteen

Memories besieged Amelia as she approached the sprawling city of Sydney. It had been less than two months since she'd lived and worked in the city, and yet it seemed like a lifetime ago. How trapped she'd felt! Chills crept up her spine. Nowhere had felt safe because she'd lived and worked in the less salubrious suburbs, not by choice, but because as soon as the better establishments saw her résumé, she was told not to call them, they'd call her. She knew what that meant. No one in the posh northern suburbs or even the city centre wanted to hire someone from the lower socioeconomic suburbs. It was Kings Cross or back in the burbs.

Water's Edge had become her haven. Her place of safety. Of rest. She comforted herself knowing she would return soon. However, even that did little to calm her heart's painful thudding whenever she thought about meeting her mother.

Her hands gripped the steering wheel as she turned off the

M4 and headed down Drury Road. Her mother's apartment building was in a suburb renown for robberies and drug dealing, as well as all other forms of debauchery. Though she'd grown used to navigating rough-and-tumble places, the thought of her mother living in this area alone made her throat close. Not that having her father around would have offered any protection.

It was all so familiar. Run-down shops, broken-down fences, long-condemned houses that somehow remained standing. The Roaring Bull pub. A shiver as cold as ice ran through her. She couldn't even look at that feral place without feeling nauseous.

How blessed she was to have gotten out of here.

Lord God, thank You for Your many blessings. I truly don't deserve the new life You've given me, but I'm so very thankful for it. Please go with me now as I meet my mother. Give me the right words and the right attitude. Help me to share with her the hope I've found in You.

She pulled up to the kerb alongside the apartment building. The exterior had been in sore need of paint when she'd last been there. Now, whatever icky-brown paint was left was peeling off. Rubbish overflowing from a skip bin littered the ground, and a group of men sat on the steps smoking cigarettes and drinking beer.

She fell back into observing the safety procedures that had become second nature to her when she'd lived here. Grasping the pepper spray tucked into her jacket pocket as she locked her car, she scanned the area for a clear route to the second level. The side staircase would allow her to skirt around the men. She ignored their catcalls and hurried up the steps to her mother's apartment.

By the time she reached the fifth floor, she could barely

breathe. She'd forgotten how heavy the air was here. So different to the clean, fresh ocean air of Water's Edge.

Hovering on the balcony, she uttered another short prayer before rapping on the door. The shuffling on the other side seemed to last for an eternity before it opened.

When her mother appeared, Amelia's chest tightened at her diminutive form. Much of her frailness was clearly due to illness, but years of smoking and taking drugs had given her deteriorated state a head start. Her hair was greyer than she remembered. Thinner, too. In addition to the lines years of smoking had carved around her mouth, wrinkles that came with age had now also appeared, making her look much older than fifty-seven. She pulled her threadbare bathrobe tighter over her pyjamas, shifting on stocking-clad feet.

"Well, there you are, Amelia. I wasn't sure you'd come." Her voice was raspy. Weak.

"I told you I would."

"Telling me you would never meant anything before." A bout of coughing racked her body. "You'd tell me you were staying, and then you'd be gone a week later."

"That was a long time ago, Mum." A gentleness within Amelia ached to touch her mum's hand, maybe even kiss her cheek.

In the past, she would have retorted by saying that, when she did stay, they always ended up arguing. But now, there was no reason to remind her of that, to waste energy on the past—especially since energy was something her mother seemed short on.

"Can we go inside and sit?" Amelia asked, not because she wished to, but because her mother could barely stand.

Her mother hesitated before stepping aside. "I didn't have a chance to clean the house before you came."

Mustiness hung in the air suggesting the windows hadn't been opened for weeks, perhaps months. Amelia glanced around the single-bedroom apartment. Her mother had never been houseproud, but she'd not let it get to this state before. Amelia's mouth went dry as an oxygen tank and a box of medical supplies told her how ill her mother was. Although never in the best of health, she'd always been a fighter who somehow managed to get through whatever came her way. Not this time.

Moving a pile of newspapers and mail aside, Amelia settled on the couch across from the armchair her mother dropped into. The blanket, magazines, water glass, dirty dishes, and TV remote suggested she spent most of her time there.

She placed a crocheted blanket over her legs before her cool blue eyes settled on Amelia. "So, why'd you come?"

Of course, her mother would be on the attack. Amelia expected no less.

But where to begin? Did she explain she came because she had no room for malice in her life after being forgiven by Jesus? Did she dare try to share how He'd transformed her life? Or should she focus on the fact that her mother had reached out to her, her way of asking for help, something she rarely did? Though she wouldn't ask for assistance directly, initiating contact was a silent cry. But being proud, she'd never admit it.

Amelia took a deep breath. "It was wrong of me to stay away for as long as I did. I should have reached out to you long before you called me."

Her mother blinked, cocked her head to one side, frowned. "You don't sound like yourself."

A bittersweet smile wrenched Amelia's mouth. "It's because I'm different now, Mum. Everything's different."

Her mother slumped back, her lips twisting. "Things don't change so easily. We're all on the path life has dealt us, and we stay on it. Different, ha! You're deluded."

Amelia had wondered how the confirmation that she should take the plunge and describe the way the Lord had redeemed her would look. Now she knew. "I'm not crazy, Mum. I truly am different." She leaned towards her mother. "Will you listen if I tell you what's happened to me in the past couple of months?"

"So long as you don't tell me you've had some kind of religious experience." She raised a brow and pinned Amelia with her gaze.

Had she heard? No, she couldn't possibly have. Amelia had no contact with anyone her mother would know. What was she to do?

How could she stay quiet when she'd experienced the most life-changing event ever and longed to share the gospel message with her mother before it was too late? She *needed* to share what had happened to her. Explain why she was different and tell her *she* also could be transformed inwardly, even though her outer body was decaying. If Amelia didn't say it, she may as well have not come.

But then the verses Willow gave her before she left came to her. 1 John 3, verses 16 to 18. *This is how we know what love is: Jesus Christ laid down His life for us. And we ought to lay down our lives for our brothers and sisters. If anyone has material possessions and sees a brother or sister in need but has no pity on them, how can the love of God be in that person? Dear children, let us not love with words or speech but with actions and in truth.*

She needed to follow her words with action. She needed to love her mother, not just preach to her. *Lord, please help me....*

Her stomach fluttered as if butterflies had been set loose. Shouldn't sharing the single most important event she'd ever experienced be easy? Why did it seem so hard?

Be alert and of sober mind. Your enemy the devil prowls around like a roaring lion looking for someone to devour.

That was it. The devil didn't want her to share. He didn't want to lose her mother to the Lord, not when she was so close to being his forever.

Okay, Lord, let's do this. I trust You to help me speak with love and humility, not judgement or haughtiness. Soften my mother's heart, Lord, that she might see You.

She took her mother's thin hand, cold flesh limp beneath her touch. Although her mother flinched, she didn't withdraw her hand from under Amelia's.

"Mum, please just listen, okay?"

Her mother shrugged. "Go ahead."

Amelia swallowed hard. "When I arrived in Water's Edge, I found work in a bar."

"Nothing different there." Coughs racked her mother's body again.

"Can I get you something? Fresh water? Medicine?"

She shook her head. The coughing finally eased.

"Like I was saying, I found work in a bar. Water's Edge is the cutest little town, Mum. You should see it." But then Amelia recalled the bar, and her smile slipped.

"I've worked in a lot of unsavoury places, but this bar was

soul-crushing. It probably wasn't any worse than any other, but I was at rock bottom. I'd had enough. I wanted a change, but I had no idea how to go about it. That's when I met Charlotte."

Her mother's eyes narrowed. "Charlotte, huh?"

Amelia nodded. "She's a kind woman who owns the Water's Edge diner. She found me outside the bar one night, distraught and lost, and invited me to church. She didn't care that I reeked of cigarette smoke or wore clothes better suited to a bartender than a churchgoer. She took me as I was, and that night, I asked Jesus to do the same."

Her mother stiffened. Drew back. "And why would you do that?"

"My life was meaningless. Deep down in my soul, I was empty, and no matter what city or town I moved to, no matter what bar I worked in or what people I associated with, nothing gave me meaning or purpose or the answers to life I longed for. It took hitting rock bottom to realise I was searching for God all along. In Him, I found meaning, purpose, forgiveness, and unconditional love."

Amelia's heart pounded. Never would she have had the confidence to speak with her mother like this before. God truly was with her.

But how would her mother respond?

Amelia didn't have long to wait.

Contempt snarled up her mother's thin lips as she snatched her hand away. "Forgiveness? From someone you can't see? How on earth is that supposed to fulfil you?"

Pressing her hands together, Amelia prayed silently for the right words. "I might not see Him in front of me, Mum, but His hand has been over every step I've taken since I asked Him into my life. You wouldn't believe the things that have happened.

"Charlotte gave me a job at the diner, and she fixed me up with a fantastic roommate who's helping me grow in my faith every day. Her parents are just as wonderful as she is, and her brother..." How could mere words capture all she felt for Lucas? Her heart beat faster at the thought of him. "He's the most wonderful person I've ever known."

"So that's it. You've found a man. I knew there had to be a solid reason for your head being in the clouds."

Amelia bit her lip. She wouldn't let her mother's cynicism affect her. "My feet are more firmly planted than they've ever been. Lucas isn't like the selfish men from before who only wanted one thing from me. He's the kindest, gentlest man you'll ever meet. I have peace and purpose now. I know you think I'm crazy, but meeting God has been the best thing that's happened to me—ever. He's changing me from the inside out. And He can do the same for you."

Her mother bristled, her expression hardening and her back stiffening. "If you haven't noticed, I'm reaching the end of my life." She swept a hand before her body. "It's too late for me. Besides, I've no need for a god I can't see."

Every bit of Amelia deflated. Was this the end? It couldn't be.

She took her mother's hand again and squeezed it. "It's never too late, Mum. It doesn't matter how much or how little time you have left. God's always there. His door is always open wide. It's His greatest joy when His wayward children turn to Him. Trust me, if there's anything I've learned since giving my life to Christ, it's that it's never too late. For anyone. Not while they have breath."

"Yes, well. I don't have much of that left."

"I know." The cold from her mother's hand seemed to reach inside Amelia's chest and grab on tight. "How—how much time have they said you have?"

Her mother faced her, her eyes filling. "Not long. Months. Maybe weeks."

"Oh, Mum." Amelia scooted closer and embraced her. Her frame, so birdlike, felt as if one tight hug could break her, leaving Amelia afraid to hurt her. "I'm so sorry," she whispered against her mother's ear, the familiar overly sweet scent of her cheap shampoo no longer obscured by cigarette odour.

"There's nothing to be done about it."

Amelia drew back. "But surely the chemo might work?"

Her mother shook her head. Another bout of coughing engulfed her. "They said it might give me a little longer, that's all."

A heavy invisible weight crushed Amelia's shoulders. Despite their turbulent relationship, knowing her mother was dying tore at her heart. "I'll be here for you, Mum. I'm sorry I didn't come sooner."

"I don't expect you to stay."

"But I want to. You're my mother. How can I not be here for you?"

Her mother lifted a shaky hand to Amelia's cheek and gave the tiniest of smiles. "My sweet girl."

Oh. As she placed her hand over her mother's, tears built behind Amelia's eyes, and a pinprick of hope lifted her. Had

God heard her prayer? Her mother's gesture was such a small step, but it *was* a step.

Lord, thank You for filling me with love and compassion for my mum. Draw her to Yourself, dear Lord, and use me in whatever way You see fit.

※

Lucas unlocked his phone for the hundredth time in the past hour. Determined as he was to wait until he heard from Amelia, the temptation to call her was strong. While he wished she'd allowed him to go with her, he understood. This was something she needed to do on her own, but the reunion could go awry. He'd been praying for her since she left.

Turning back to the wall of the Youth Centre's recreation room, he picked up the paint roller once more. Adam had gone home hours earlier, but Lucas couldn't bring himself to leave. He needed a task to focus on. Sure, the vacant building's silence and solitude could leave too much room for his thoughts, but he needed to linger somewhere where hopes and dreams outweighed that fear.

He'd just finished the second coat when the front door swooshed open. He smiled, figuring it was Adam. "Couldn't resist joining me, could you?"

"No, I couldn't."

His heart leapt. Amelia? He whirled to face her, crossing the room to take her in his arms. "Sweetheart," he murmured into her hair. "Am I glad to see you."

She clung to him. He held her for many moments, only breaking apart when she stepped back. With a sigh, she reached up and cupped his cheek. "And I'm so happy to see you. It's only been one day, but it feels like an eternity."

He placed a tender kiss on her lips. "I know. Come sit."

They made their way, hand-in-hand, to a stack of plywood. He faced her once they were seated. "How was it?"

Her gaze dropped to their hands. When her gaze met his, tears had pooled in her eyes.

"Was it that terrible?"

She shook her head. "Just difficult. Emotional."

He nodded. "I'm sure."

A silence followed.

"How's your mum?"

Her brown eyes glazing, she stared ahead and kicked her feet back and forth as if needing to expel pent-up energy. "Different. I never imagined she could look so frail. It's like life has had its way with her and this is what's left. It's so sad."

With no need for words, he waited, the hold he kept on her hands confirming he wasn't going anywhere.

"I told her I found God and there's hope for her as well. She could make her peace with Him. And with me." Her lips trembled. "I forgave her for everything and told her I want to spend time with her."

"Wow. How did she handle all that?"

"I don't think she knew what to do with it. I probably overloaded her, but the walls between us came down." She sniffled, sucked in a jagged breath.

"That had to be worth it, then."

Her shoulders curved inward, and she shivered. "She doesn't have long to live, and she's all alone." She lifted her gaze to his.

"I can't imagine the despair she's feeling. And to think she's going through this without hope in God..."

When she tugged her hands away to cover her face, he wrapped his arms around her shoulders and held her, letting her sob against his chest. "It's a good thing she called you." He stroked her hair. "I've heard it said that sometimes we're the only Bible a person will ever read."

She pulled back and wiped her tears with her sleeve before blinking up at him. "You mean, because we're called to represent Him?"

"Exactly." He fished a tissue from his pocket and passed it over. "Not everyone discovers Christ by reading the Bible. That comes, but sometimes a tangible demonstration of His mercy and grace will lead a person to Him. The way you've allowed the Lord to transform your heart will speak to your mother. More than that, it'll give her hope because you're a living, breathing representation of His redemption and she knows better than anyone all you've had to overcome."

He leaned forward, resting his forehead against hers as his heart broke a little. Though she hadn't said anything yet, he sensed his sweetheart's reunion with her mother would mean he'd need to give her up in some form, at least for a time, and that thought tightened a cord around his heart. "What are you going to do now?"

She found his hands and squeezed them. "I need to be there for her. I know that much."

The cord tightened further. Yep. He'd been right. "Yes, of course, you do."

She ran her thumb along the top of his hand, studying their intertwined fingers. "The only logical thing is to move close to her, at least for the time being. She's going to need more help as time goes by, and it'll do little good if I'm so far away I can't get to her quickly."

"That makes sense."

Her chin rose as resolve overtook the look of helplessness she'd worn. "I said I'd stay with her as long as she needs me to. I want to make the time she has left more comfortable."

He breathed deeply as he gazed into her eyes. "When do you need to go?" Despite the heaviness in his heart, he kept his voice level. While he wanted nothing more than to hold her and keep her to himself, that was selfish. Her mother needed her. He had to let her go.

Her shoulders drooped. "As soon as possible. I'll have to let Dr. Turner and Charlotte know I won't be back at work for a while."

"They'll understand. We're all behind you, sweetheart."

Her smile wobbled. "I know it's not far, but deep down, I don't want to leave, especially now I feel like I've found my home."

"We'll all be here waiting for you." He ran his finger down her hairline. "Water's Edge, the Youth Centre..."

A lump formed in his stomach. "You're planning on coming back, aren't you?"

She reached out and stroked his cheek. "Of course, I am. You think the reason I don't want to leave is because I'll miss Water's Edge. I will, but the part of town I can't bear the thought of leaving is you. I don't want to leave you, Lucas."

Air whooshed from his lungs. Her words were like a stream of warm honey. He gathered her in his arms again, lowered his mouth to hers, and kissed her deeply.

Finally releasing her, he cupped her cheeks and gazed into her eyes. "I'm not going anywhere, Amelia. I'll be here waiting for you."

She drew in a deep breath, blinking rapidly as if fighting emotion. "Knowing that will make it easier to bear."

"You need to do this, sweetheart, but I don't believe God brought us together only to tear us apart. You won't be far away, but even when the distance feels like a trial, we can trust that God's doing a good work in us. He finishes everything He starts. You know that, don't you?"

"I do." She nestled a soft cheek closer into his palm. "I'd never be able to face this without Him. But part of me wants to hold on to you with all I'm worth."

He forced himself to smile. Although he felt the same, he needed to be strong for her. He angled his head. "What's the old adage?"

"Absence makes the heart grow fonder...." They finished it together, sharing a smile before he once again lowered his mouth and kissed her thoroughly.

Chapter Fourteen

"I can't take all these clothes," Amelia protested for the tenth time since she started packing.

"It's only three outfits," Willow countered. "I haven't worn them in weeks. You should take them."

"You haven't worn them because they've been in my wardrobe." Chuckling, Amelia shook her head at her friend.

Though Willow smiled, sadness lingered in her eyes. "I want you to take them. Please?"

Amelia huffed as she tucked them into her suitcase. "If you insist. I guess it'll be nice to have a little reminder of you while I'm gone."

Willow dropped onto the bed, toying with the cover of a book Amelia had yet to pack. "Don't be a stranger, hey?"

"Don't worry. I'll be visiting so much you'll be sick of me."

"That would be impossible."

Amelia frowned. What was this? *Willow* sounding melancholy? "Is something wrong?"

Willow hesitated before waving off the question with one hand. "It's nothing."

"No." Amelia crossed her arms. "I know you too well by now to let you get away with that. Talk."

Willow's long sigh ruffled her bouncy hair. "I keep thinking about you and Lucas. Things have fallen into place, and I'd hate for anything to jeopardise what you've got."

Amelia's chest tightened. Willow had verbalised her exact feelings. Although she felt secure in Lucas's love, who knew what time apart would do to a new relationship? The old adage might be right, but it also might not be. Jutting up her chin, she put on a brave face. "I'm going to Sydney, not the moon. Like I said, I'll be back often. And you two can come up if you get a hankering for city life."

Straightening, Willow pulled her knees to her chest. "I must sound awfully selfish. I'm glad you've got a chance to mend things with your mum. I can't imagine not having a good relationship with mine."

"I'm glad, too. Our relationship is far from mended," Amelia admitted. "But the walls have come down, and that's more than I ever dreamed possible. She needs practical help. A lot of it. That might develop to the point where we can discuss spiritual things, too."

"God will open the doors to share with her. I'm sure of it."

He'd already paved the way. She had no doubt He was at work on her mother, even now.

"The house will feel lonely without you here." Willow bounced a bit on the bed. "But don't worry. I'm holding your bedroom until you get back." A mischievous grin stretched her lips, and her eyes shone. "Unless you're ready for a new roommate by then. Namely, a husband..."

"Willow!" Amelia snatched a pillow and tossed it in her direction, hitting her square in the face.

Willow erupted into laughter, though she attempted to appear taken aback. "Don't tell me the idea doesn't appeal to you."

Amelia zipped up her suitcase before joining Willow on the bed. "It does. I'm just trying not to think too much about what I want for the future. If I do and it doesn't turn out the way I think it should or want it to, I might get bitter, and that's the last thing I want when there's so much evidence of God's grace in my life. My plan is to entrust everything to Him, do what He's called me to do, and see where it goes."

Willow beamed. "You're going to do just fine. As much as I hate to see you go, I'll help you with your luggage. But remember, you didn't pack everything. I expect you back soon, Amelia Anderson."

"You can count on it." Heart constricting, Amelia leaned closer and drew her in for a hug.

"Looks like we're all set." Lucas glanced over the last of the details for the Youth Centre's opening day. It was late, but he'd decided to drop the finishing touches by Samuel's office instead of waiting until morning.

Ten days after Amelia left to be with her mother in Sydney, the final tasks on the centre had been completed. Things wouldn't have been finished quite so swiftly had he not been doing everything he could to distract himself from the void she'd left. Although they talked often on the phone, it did little to ease the ache of separation.

"It's going to be an exciting day—that's for sure," Samuel remarked. "I don't think I've seen the kids so hyper."

"I can't wait for them to experience what we have in store." Lucas smiled at their—and *his*—anticipation. "Thanks again for helping with the planning. I know you're a busy man."

Samuel grunted. "Busier now I'm working solo again. It's quiet around here without Amelia. It was nice having her help. I hardly know how I managed before she came."

Lucas's throat tightened. He didn't know how *he'd* managed, either. "We're missing her on the worship team, too." Though he did his best to remain absorbed in checking over the list of details in his hand, he couldn't avoid meeting Samuel's gaze eventually.

When he did, the compassionate understanding on the elderly doctor's face touched him. "The separation won't last forever. Every couple deals with distance at some point. You're getting it out of the way early."

"That's a nice way to think about it." Lucas gave a small chuckle before sobering. "I want to believe we'll make it through this."

"You will."

How could he be so confident? Lucas exhaled heavily. "I know she needed to go, but it's frustrating to be separated during such a formative part of our relationship. What if she decides not to come back?"

Samuel clamped his hand on Lucas's shoulder. "She'll be

back, son. I'm not an expert on women, but I saw the way she looks at you."

He was right. The way she looked at him sent his heart spinning. "I told her God wouldn't start something and fail to complete it. Now here I am doubting it myself."

Samuel squeezed Lucas's shoulder. "Don't be too hard on yourself. Distance adds a new dimension to any relationship. But God has a purpose—something for both of you to learn during this time. Remain open to it."

"I will. Thanks for the reminder."

"You're more than welcome."

The aroma of freshly brewed coffee awakened Amelia's senses before she'd even poured a cup. Her mouth watered at the bacon crackling in the pan as she served scrambled eggs onto two plates and then proceeded to butter toast. She pulled a jar of jam she'd purchased the day before from the cupboard. Her mother had always been partial to raspberry preserves, so the gesture couldn't hurt when it came to mending bridges.

Since her return to Sydney, she'd thought a lot about the past. These shared pieces of years gone by were something she and her mother could bond over, something uniting them despite the chasm of things separating them.

"Something smells good."

Amelia turned with a ready smile. "You're just in time." As she helped her mother onto a chair, her chest clenched at her laboured breathing. She'd become increasingly winded during the past week or so, wheezing even in the short distance from her bedroom to the kitchen. Amelia's companionship helped the time pass more pleasantly, but her mother grew frailer with each day. Each time Amelia noted it, it reminded her to appreciate every moment, because she had no idea how many were left.

"You're spoiling me, you know," her mother remarked as Amelia brought over their plates and returned to grab the coffee pot.

"That's my intention." Amelia chuckled, filling their cups before sitting. As well as caring for her mum, she'd cleaned the small apartment top to toe and bought a new yellow tablecloth and some fresh flowers to cheer the place up.

"What will I do once you're gone?" The melancholy in her mother's voice pulled at Amelia's heart.

She touched her mum's thin wrist. The gesture would have felt foreign and stilted only weeks earlier. "Who said anything about me going? I plan to be in your hair for quite a while yet."

A new softness smoothed the cares from her mother's face. "I can't believe you picked up everything and moved here. Don't you miss your new life in Water's Edge? Though I don't understand how a girl like you could be happy in such a small town, you sound attached to the place."

"I am attached to it." Amelia rubbed her thumb over her mother's wrist, trying to ignore the bones her finger bumped against. "But I want to be here with you. Lucas reminded me Water's Edge isn't going anywhere and it'll be there whenever I get back."

Her mother toyed with her breakfast. "Tell me about him."

Warmth filled Amelia as she let herself dwell on his image.

"We only started dating recently. He's my roommate's brother. He's also the worship leader and youth pastor at church." That warmth buoyed her as she lifted her gaze. "He's the most incredible man I've ever met. He's so selfless and has such a heart for kids. He's also heading up the construction of the Youth Centre." She shook her head. "I never imagined a man like him existed, much less would show interest in me."

"He sounds too good to be true."

"I know. It helped to fish in a good pond. Not that I was fishing." Letting go of her mum's wrist, Amelia scooted back in her chair.

Her mum cocked her head. "What do you mean?"

"We met at church, not a bar."

"Oh."

Amelia wrapped her hands around her coffee mug and sighed out her contentment. How blessed she was to have met him.

"Well, I'm glad you've found a good man."

Amelia nodded. "I feel very fortunate."

"That must be a nice feeling."

Her wistfulness tugged at Amelia. "I'm sorry you never found a good man, Mum."

"I guess I never fished in a good pond." Shrugging, her mother stirred her coffee.

Amelia shifted closer and placed her hand on her mother's bony thigh. "It's not too late to meet a Man who'll never let you down."

"What are you talking about?" Her mother's head jerked up. "I'm dying. Did you forget that?"

"I'm not talking about a physical man."

"Not that hogwash again, hey." Her eyes narrowed. Hardened.

Oh Lord, soften her heart. I so much want her to know You.

"Sorry, Mum. But it's not hogwash. My relationship with Jesus is more real than anything I've ever known, even than my relationship with Lucas. He's slowly but surely transforming the way I see things, bringing meaning into every corner of my life." She held her gaze steady as she looked into her mother's eyes. "You know better than anyone the direction I was headed in. The changes the Lord has brought about for me, practically and inwardly, have made Him more tangible and closer than I could ever have imagined."

Her mother sat in silence.

Lucas had said it wasn't her job to convert a person. That was the Holy Spirit's job. She simply had to share her experience and be a living witness of the transformation God had wrought in her life through her actions and attitudes and leave the rest with Him.

Let your light shine before others, that they may see your good deeds and glorify your Father in heaven.

Now, she prayed she could fulfil that instruction and God would have the Holy Spirit at work in her mother's heart.

Finally, her mother responded, "I'm happy for you, but I'm not sure it's something I can pursue after everything that's happened."

Unbidden tears burned Amelia's eyes. "It's all right. There's time. I'm not trying to convince you to believe one way or another. I want you to know that. But I also want you to know I'm open to talking about it whenever you wish."

Her mother held her gaze before dropping it and placing

her hands around her coffee cup. "Guess I sat too long on this. It's cold."

Pushing to her feet, Amelia stood and took both their mugs. "Not to worry. There's more where that came from."

As she filled their cups with fresh coffee, she prayed for patience and for faith to trust God to do His work in her mother, in His time, in His way.

Chapter Fifteen

Lucas dragged his feet as he entered the diner. In the month since Amelia left, he hadn't gotten used to her absence. She might have been the diner's newest addition, but the place wasn't the same without her.

"Hey there, Lucas." Charlotte waved a pie knife in his direction before placing a generous slice of lemon meringue onto a plate. "Take a seat anywhere, and I'll be right over with coffee."

With peppy music playing low over the speakers and the ocean glimmering beyond the windows, the place could perk anyone up—unless it reminded them of what they were missing. He nodded to a few regulars before settling into a booth. The Youth Centre was about ready for the grand opening, and he'd spent the greater part of the morning completing last-minute odds and ends. He hadn't realised he'd skipped breakfast until his stomach began to protest.

By the time Charlotte arrived with the coffee and a piece of pie, his taste buds were set on a hamburger and fries.

"Glad you came in," she said.

"A guy's gotta eat sometime."

She studied him with a narrow gaze. "You're not looking so good, Lucas."

He blinked before laughing. "Thanks. I'm glad I can count on you to be honest."

Setting aside the coffee pot, she slid into the seat across from him and braced her forearms on the timber tabletop. "Don't get me wrong. I can tell you're content. The Youth Centre's coming along, and when you lead worship on Sundays, I feel blessed. You seem happy. But I've known you long enough to recognise that you're pining."

That was quite the word. He crossed his arms, arched a brow. "Pining? Really?"

She nodded. "You've not pined over anyone before. It's plain as day you're missing Amelia."

He lifted his hands to the ceiling. "Guilty as charged. But she's where she's supposed to be, and we talk often."

Charlotte angled her head. "When was the last time you *saw* each other?"

Ducking his head, he toyed with his pie. "Two weeks ago."

"Not often enough for young folks like you."

With the perfect blend of meringue and lemon on his fork—like the woman before him, an exemplary blend of tart and sweetness—he pointed it at her. "You're a real meddler. Has anyone told you that?"

"Often." She beamed, then swept a crumb from the table. "Do you want to know what I think you should do?"

"Whether I do or not, I'm going to find out, aren't I?"

Letting the full fork rest back on his plate, he grinned at her seriousness.

"Yes, you are. My advice is to marry that girl."

Whoa. His eyes widened. "Is it now?" Sure, he'd thought about marriage. He'd even alluded to it on the night he asked Amelia if he could court her. But they'd been dating less than two months. How could he consider marriage so soon?

Charlotte wagged a plump finger at him. "Don't let her get away."

"I don't intend to." He did his best to maintain a nonchalant demeanour. "I'm waiting until we don't have so much on our plates."

Charlotte gestured to the plate before him. "One thing this diner has taught me is empty plates are just there to get washed and filled back up—fast. Life is no different. It's filled with busyness and challenges. If we waited for empty plates, we'd never do a thing." She leaned closer, rumpling her red apron against the booth. "That girl is as sweet as that pie now filling your plate, and like my pies and cooking, she's the best thing that ever could be added to your plate."

He released a dry chuckle. "Believe me, I know."

Reaching across the table, she grasped his wrist. "Invite her back to Water's Edge—and soon. Make sure she knows you want her around."

"I was going to invite her to the Youth Centre's opening day," he replied.

Charlotte patted his hand. "Perfect."

He shook his head, attempting to conceal his grin but failing. "Do you badger all your customers this way?"

153

"Only the ones I like the best," she replied with a wink. "You remember what I said, okay?"

He inclined his head, mock saluting her. "Yes, ma'am."

The bell above the door jingled as a party of six filed into the diner.

"Looks like those folks saved you from my further pestering." With a slap on the table, she slid out of the booth. "What're you having for lunch, hun?"

"Hamburger and fries, please."

"Coming right up." She winked again before bustling over to greet the new arrivals.

Left alone, Lucas toyed with his paper napkin and cutlery and pondered Charlotte's advice. He'd felt God's peace about moving forward with Amelia for some time, but should he take the leap and propose?

Charlotte was right—there was never a perfect time to do anything. Something would always be happening in his and Amelia's lives. But wasn't it too soon? They hadn't had time to truly get to know each other.

But he knew her enough to know he wanted to spend the rest of his life with her. The time apart had convinced him she made him happy. She lit up his life. Made him laugh. Warmed his heart.

He loved her.

He swallowed hard. But was he ready to act? Besides, she needed to spend as much uninterrupted time with her mother as possible.

He'd wait until he felt sure the Lord was guiding him forward.

For now, he'd invite her to the Youth Centre opening. There'd be no greater blessing than having her by his side at such an important event. Other than marrying her, of course. But that would need to wait.

By the time her mother turned in for the night, Amelia was exhausted. Although she should be asleep, she ventured onto the small balcony and breathed in the evening air. Settling into a plastic chair, she shivered and pulled her cardigan tighter while two men quarrelled in the apartment below her.

Her mother's condition had grown worse, taxing them both physically and emotionally. How quickly time was slipping by, although each day seemed long. Every waking moment she spent at her mother's side, but she'd yet to share everything she wished to.

Even before coming to God, she'd heard what the Bible had to say about life being but a vapour. She'd never understood it more fully than she did now. Heaviness had settled over her soul as the days passed and her mother's heart remained closed to God. Would she die without knowing Him? He wouldn't force her to acknowledge Him as her Lord and Saviour. He would keep knocking, but *she* had to answer. How could she be so stubborn when all He wanted to do was give her a life with Him that would last for eternity? Amelia didn't understand it.

Tears flooded her eyes, blurring the lights of suburbia. As moisture slid down her cheeks, she swiped it with her hand.

She also missed Lucas, longed to be with him. That someone she hadn't known existed a short while ago could feel such a key part of her existence was incredible. Absence truly did make the heart grow fonder.

When a fresh torrent of tears hit, she let them flow. She'd tried to be strong, but right now, exhaustion left her emotionally drained.

When her phone buzzed, she wiped her tears and pulled the phone from her pocket. Lucas's name flashed on the screen, warming her.

"Hey."

"Hi, sweetheart. How are you?"

Her eyes slid shut at the rumble of his voice. "I'm okay. How are you?"

"You don't sound okay."

Was her exhaustion so obvious?

With his tone so tender, emotion thickened her throat, making the words hard to push out. "I–I don't know what's wrong with me. I'm so weepy. Everything feels... hard."

"Because it is." His tenderness wrapped around her, hugging her through the distance. "Caring for a terminally ill loved one isn't easy. Apart from that, you uprooted your life and made a move you weren't expecting. Give yourself a little grace."

Her heart melted. "The worst part"—she had to pause when her voice caught in her thick throat—"is being away from you."

"I feel the same."

How she longed to see him. To hold him. Kiss him.

"How's your mum?" he asked.

She exhaled. "I never imagined anything could be so bittersweet. If a couple of weeks ago you'd told me I'd be talking as openly with her as I do now, I would have called you crazy. She's softer, more receptive, than she's ever been."

"Perhaps you are as well."

Good point. She rubbed her forehead. "I wish we'd made amends years ago, not when she's about to die." Swallowing hard, she switched her phone to her other ear and hugged her knees to her chest. "But tell me, how are things with you? I want to hear all the news."

"You can pretty much guess the usual. Game nights at the Kelleys' are still a riot. Charlotte's still butting into the business of everyone who sits in a booth at the diner.... Just the ordinary."

Amelia sighed. "Ordinary, maybe, but nothing sounds more heavenly."

"There's one thing I have to tell you that doesn't happen every day." His voice perked up. "A date's been set for the Youth Centre opening."

"Fantastic! I can't believe it's finally happening. The whole town must be buzzing."

"It is. We're doing our best to ensure it's a time of celebration for everyone, especially those who've been involved in the building." He cleared his throat. "That includes you, Amelia."

"Oh, I didn't do much."

"But you did." He grew silent.

She was about to ask if he was all right when he continued.

"You know, I didn't realise it at first, but as you stepped in to help, you became an inextricable part of its makeup. Your generosity and love for people lit up the place even though it was only half-finished. You brought the kind of light I want the centre to exemplify."

She scolded herself as a fresh onslaught of tears threatened. It felt ages since she'd been close enough to swing by the centre any day of the week and assist with odds and ends, whether it was painting or sorting the donations of toys and supplies shared by the town's citizens. "Thank you. That's a lovely compliment."

"I mean it." He hesitated again. "I know you're busy, and I don't want to impose on your time with your mum. But I'd love you to come to the opening day. It's this coming Saturday. But only if you feel comfortable leaving—"

"Of course, I'll come. I wouldn't miss it for the world," she interrupted, her heart swelling with excitement for both the opening and seeing the man she loved.

He let out a little whoop. "I'm so happy to hear that, and I know the rest of the town will be too. The opening wouldn't be the same without you there."

"I can't wait to see you, Lucas."

"I can't wait to see you more."

A tingle ran through her as she imagined the touch of his hand and the taste of his lips. "Not possible."

"Let's call it a tie then, shall we?"

She sank back into her chair, the former tension draining. "Yes, let's."

"You sound tired. I'll let you go so you can get some sleep. I'll talk to you tomorrow?"

Her heart sank. Could she part from the comfort of his voice so soon? She twisted her grip on the phone. She'd better.

She was nearly falling asleep in her chair. "Yes, you will. Goodnight, Lucas."

"Goodnight, sweetheart."

Any other night, the anticipation of the opening and seeing Lucas would have kept her awake, but she was practically asleep by the time her head hit the pillow, leaving thoughts of the centre—and him—to the following day.

Chapter Sixteen

※

Lucas had been certain the long-awaited Youth Centre opening day would be a popular affair, but the turnout stunned him. The cloudless day complied, sun warming the area, and by noon, the entire centre brimmed with parents chasing after excited children and teens playing basketball and volleyball on the outdoor courts.

Despite how wonderful this was, Amelia's presence at the refreshment booth near the entrance thrilled him most. When his gaze settled on her, she was bending forward, handing an ice-cream cone to a small boy. She looked up after finishing the transaction and sent Lucas a smile that reached deep inside him and made his heart pound. The queue for refreshments had died down, and he was about to stride right over and kiss the woman who was driving him mad in the best possible way when his dad joined him.

"Well done, son." Pride widened his dad's broad smile.

"I couldn't have done it without your help."

"I'm not so sure about that." He held out a plastic cup. "I brought you some ginger beer."

"Thanks." Lucas accepted the cup and gave a salute with it. The cool, sweet beverage was more than welcome, and he downed it in a few gulps. The sound of the sea faded into the background as he returned his attention to the crowd and a strange panic settled in his stomach. The day was a huge success, but it was only one day. What would happen in the days, weeks, and months ahead? Could all the programs and facilities be maintained into the future? Had he bitten off more than he could chew?

He'd envisioned the centre for so long that wondering now if it could remain beneficial for the children he sought to enrich seemed out of place.

"Something on your mind?" Dad sipped his own ginger beer.

Lucas exhaled. He'd never been good at concealing worry. "Just last-minute doubts."

"About?" His dad angled his head, lifted a brow.

"What if I can't keep it all going? If I let the kids down?"

"Oh. I see. Carrying it yourself now, are you?"

Ouch. Lucas grimaced and released a breath. "Caught out in one."

His dad clapped him on the back. "Easy to do, son. You want to do everything you can to impact their lives—and I know you will—but ultimately, the kids are in God's care. This is His project, not yours. You need to trust Him to finish what He's started."

With a deep breath, Lucas swirled the dregs of liquid in his cup. They lost their pep and fizz as they spun around to no avail, just as he'd almost done. "You're right. Thanks for the reminder."

"Anytime." His dad grinned. "Good to see Amelia here today."

Lucas's gaze swung back to the refreshment stand. A queue had formed once again, and the sweet lilt of her laugh floated to his ears on the warm breeze. "I've been missing her a lot."

"We know."

"I keep reminding myself God brought her to Water's Edge for a purpose and orchestrated this reunion with her mother for a reason, but that doesn't stop me from wanting to keep her close."

"I'm glad she's reunited with her mother. It would have been heartbreaking for her to pass without them reconciling."

"Absolutely. It hasn't been easy for Amelia, but mending bridges has been rewarding, although she's emotionally exhausted."

"I can only imagine how much."

His gaze lingered on her before he turned back to his father. "I want to marry her, Dad."

His dad's eyes widened, then crinkled with his broad smile. "That's the best news I've heard all day. Your mum and I always knew, one day, God would bring the right woman into your life. We just had to be patient. You don't need our blessing, but I want you to know you have our full support. She's a wonderful girl."

Lucas's throat closed. "I'll always need and want the blessing of both you and Mum, no matter what I do." He embraced his dad, his heart swelling. "Thanks, Dad. For everything."

"You're welcome, son." When they broke apart, his dad

nodded towards the refreshment stand, his eyes twinkling. "I'd say your girl could use a break. Why don't you go over there and take a walk around the centre? You both deserve to enjoy the festivities as much as anyone."

Lucas didn't need to be asked twice. He smiled at his father before making his way towards Amelia, still barely able to believe she was here. He'd already known he wanted to spend the rest of his life with her. Receiving affirmation from his father settled that desire deeper in his heart.

But would she agree?

And what about her mum? Would she think it was too much, too soon?

It was time to find out.

He'd just about reached her when Samuel stepped into his path.

Lucas tried to get around him, but the elderly doctor seemed intent on having a chat. "What an amazing day it's been. You should be very happy."

Lucas smiled. "I am. God has blessed us greatly."

"All these families—and not all of them are from the church. This centre is the best thing that's happened to Water's Edge in a long time. God's going to use it to not only minister to the church's youth but also to reach the unchurched. I'm so proud of you for following your dream and listening to God."

The words were a real blessing and encouragement, and Lucas said so. But not before another person relieved Amelia, and she disappeared.

It seemed everyone wanted to congratulate him. What could he do other than be polite and thank them and tell them all the glory should be given to God?

An hour later, he found her in the rec room.

***

The exhaustion of the day hit Amelia the moment she dropped into one of the kiddy chairs in the centre's recreation room. She couldn't remember ever feeling so tired and happy at the same time. Opening day had been such a success, as further evidenced by the dodgeballs, foam blocks, and colouring books scattered around the room. Smiling, she thought back on the children's joyful faces. Lucas would do an incredible job with the programs. She'd never been prouder of anyone.

"There you are."

Her heart leapt at the sight of him leaning against the doorway, his attention fixed on her. The look in his eyes said far more than his words ever could.

"I've come to rescue you."

She waved him off. "I'm just going to clean up the last of the toys in here."

He strode forward and grabbed her hand. "Adam and the guys have it from here. You've done more than your share today, and they know it. They ordered me to find you and take you away."

She laughed. Would having people look out for her interests out of sheer friendliness ever grow old? "That's nice of them."

"I bet you haven't eaten all day." He guided her down the hallway.

"I did so," she protested.

"Oh yeah? What?"

"An ice cream and a handful of popcorn."

"Delicious as that sounds, we can do better than that."

Wobbling on her feet, she had to agree. Her blood sugar needed a serious boost. "You'll get no fight from me."

"I know a good place." The grin he tossed her made her pulse race. "I've been waiting to have you to myself all day."

"Me too." Wanting to savour every moment with him, she gripped his hand tighter.

They waved to the others as they slipped through the now-quiet Youth Centre and out into the balmy evening air. "It was a beautiful day, Lucas." She looped her arm through his. "Thanks for letting me be a part of it."

Pausing, he faced her and ran two fingers down her cheek. "The way I see it, there was no other option. I've missed you, Amelia."

She rested her head on his shoulder. "I've missed you too. It's so wonderful to be back. Water's Edge was beginning to feel like home, but being away confirmed it. It's like a piece of me is missing when I'm not here."

He kissed the top of her head. "You took a piece of me with you when you left."

Gazing into his eyes, she reached up and stroked his cheek. "I didn't just take a piece of you." She pressed her hand over her heart. "It might sound silly, but I feel like you were wrapped up inside of me even when I couldn't see you."

He leaned forward and kissed her tenderly on the lips. Resting his forehead against hers, he spoke in a whisper. "It doesn't sound silly at all."

All the emotional turmoil of the past weeks was forgotten as his words curled under her skin and around her heart like a warm embrace. She snuggled into him, the warmth of his arms enveloping her. "Oh, Lucas."

They finally drew apart and walked in companionable silence to his car as she savoured the sweetness of his presence. He opened the passenger door and helped her in. When he didn't close it, she angled her head. "What is it?"

He was studying her, and though he smiled, an emotion she couldn't place stirred behind his eyes. He bent down and kissed her lips again. "Nothing. I'm just glad you're here."

Though his words warmed her heart, something cold tightened her stomach. Was something wrong?

When he remained silent during the first part of their drive, she was certain of it. She grasped his hand. "You seem out of sorts. Is it just the anticlimax after the big day?"

His smile wry, his attention remained on the road. "The most highly anticipated part of my day is yet to come."

"What do you mean?" Her pulse raced when he hesitated. "Lucas?"

He ran a restless hand over his jaw. "I wasn't planning on doing this tonight, but I feel like the time is right—it's more than right."

What did he mean? "For what?"

He kept his gaze on the road. An array of emotions chased across his face before he turned into the lookout car park. The pounding of her heart became painful now as he shut off the engine, jumped out, and strode around the car to open the passenger door. Then he helped her out, clasped her hand, and almost pulled her to the lookout where the city lights lit up the skyline. The tranquillity of those distant, twinkling lights felt incongruent as her insides continued their wild dance.

What *was* he doing? She stood beside him, studying his face, even the soothing scent of the sea failing to calm her. "Lucas?"

He stared at the lights while keeping a firm hold on her hand. "It's strange to think of how many times I've looked at those lights but never knew that you lived there—that you were walking through those streets searching, the same as me."

Her lips twisted. Why so melancholy?

He continued. "I was prepared to wait however long the Lord saw fit for the right woman to come into my life. I wasn't certain how long I'd stay in Water's Edge. Only for a season? Indefinitely? But I knew what I was called to at that moment, so I stayed." He faced her. "When you walked into my life, I wasn't expecting it. Suddenly, there I was, twitterpated as a schoolboy."

Despite the feelings circulating within her, she laughed. "You didn't seem twitterpated. More like calm and collected."

He chuckled with her before growing serious. "That wasn't my inward state. I can tell you I've never experienced those emotions for anyone. Ever."

Oh. Her heart quickened at the intensity in his eyes.

She wanted to assure him it was the same for her, but once again tongue-tied, she stood mute.

He drew her to him. The steady beating of his heart as she rested her head against his chest brought comfort to every corner of her soul. When he spoke, his voice, thick with emotion, seemed to come from somewhere deep inside him. "Not long after we met, I knew you were the one I'd been waiting for."

Closing her eyes, she felt as if she were floating.

He shifted his weight from one foot to the other before

drawing back and gazing into her eyes. "In His infinite wisdom, God saw fit to bring a woman more incredible than I could ever imagine into my world and allow dreams of the life we could have together to become deeply rooted in my heart."

As he dropped to one knee, her hand flew to her chest.

"I love you with all my heart, and I want to spend the rest of my life with you. You make my life richer. Fuller, and I'm so hoping you'll accept my proposal. Amelia Anderson, will you marry me?"

Happy tears sprang to her eyes. "Oh, Lucas. I can't believe it."

Elation burst through his laugh. "Well, believe it because I've never been surer of anything in my life."

She threw her arms around his neck, sending him toppling backwards onto the damp ground. They both laughed. She gave her answer with a deep and passionate kiss.

When they broke apart, he shook his head. "I don't have a ring. I wasn't kidding when I said I hadn't planned to do this tonight. But all at once, it felt right, and I couldn't help myself."

She rested her head on his shoulder. As she breathed in his familiar scent, she knew without a doubt that she, too, had never been surer of anything. "It doesn't matter. There's plenty of time for that. I just want to be with you."

His eyes shone. "I'll take it that's a yes?"

Swiping at the tears tickling her cheeks, she nodded. "Without a doubt, yes!"

He drew her closer and kissed her again.

Pure joy filled her as her heart tumbled over itself.

His gentle, yet callused fingertips skidded across her cheek as he smoothed a loose lock of hair off her forehead. "Now I have your answer, there's one more thing I need to do."

She tipped her head. "And what's that?"

His expression had grown serious. "Ask your mother's permission."

Oh. Her heart constricted. Would her mother agree? Not that she could stop them, but having her support would be nice.

A frown pressed his lips white. "That's all right with you, isn't it?"

"Yes, yes, of course." She hugged him tight to assure him. "I'm just taking it all in. Getting to marry you and having my mum back in my life. I couldn't ask for anything more."

He leaned in and brushed his lips against hers. She responded willingly. By the time they parted, the damp ground had soaked their jeans.

"I hope wherever we're going for dinner is all right with their patrons sporting grass stains," she joked as he helped her to her feet.

"Charlotte's never been the finicky type, so I think we're all right."

"We're going to Charlotte's?"

"I thought it only right since she'll want to know about our engagement. She's been more on my case about ensuring you don't get away than even my mother."

Looping her arm through his, Amelia chuckled. "Well, in that case, she deserves to know as soon as possible."

"Right," he agreed. "Let's bring her the good news and get you some food."

She agreed without reservation, but with all the excitement coursing through her, she somehow doubted she could eat.

Chapter Seventeen

❦

News of the engagement spread through Water's Edge like a tsunami. Though the town had already accepted Amelia with open arms, the way the people embraced her during this new and exciting stage of their lives filled him with joy. His mum, dad, and Willow were ecstatic.

"I just knew it!" Willow exclaimed the moment the announcement left his mouth. "I knew you were right for each other all along! What a happy ending!"

He did agree that the Lord had orchestrated matters in beautiful ways, but it was their beginning not their ending. And the months ahead would not be easy ones for his bride-to-be. Her mother's health wasn't improving, and her imminent passing cast a shadow over the happy news.

Although he had a great deal to do now the Youth Centre was up and running, he elected to return to Sydney with Amelia the day after the grand opening. She protested, telling him the news could wait until he wasn't so busy, but he insisted. "Ensuring your mum hears the news from us as soon as possible is what's important right now."

He apologised for how swiftly word had gotten out, saying he'd hoped to gain her mother's permission before making the official announcement.

Amelia had waved off his words. "Don't worry about that. The folks of Water's Edge have become my family, and I wouldn't dream of keeping this from them. Besides, our engagement is as good as a done deal. She'll love you. I know she will."

He had no reason to doubt her, but that didn't stop the nerves welling within him while he drove into Sydney. The tension in Amelia's hand as she held his proved he wasn't the only one.

After pulling up outside the dilapidated apartment building, they sat in silence.

She eventually faced him. "Ready?"

His gaze swept her gorgeous face. Though he'd believed it to be impossible, his love for her had already deepened. "If you are, I am."

She exhaled, her fingers tightening around his. He smiled his encouragement before climbing out of the car and coming around to the passenger's side. They clasped hands again as she led the way up the building's front steps, weaving around a group of men drinking beer.

The place's run-down state explained why she'd been so distressed about her mother living here alone. If he hadn't already been sure his fiancée had been right where she was supposed to be during the past weeks, he would have been now.

Vivian Anderson needed her daughter with her, if for no other reason than to keep her safe in her frail state.

Amelia knocked lightly on the door before opening it with a key. "Mum? It's me."

"I'm in the living room." Her voice, raspy and weak, barely reached them.

Amelia motioned for him to follow her inside. He hung back, not wishing to surprise her mother.

"Darling, it's so good to see you."

"How are you doing, Mum?"

"I'm all right. How was the opening? Did you have a good time?" A bout of coughing seized her.

Amelia waited until the bout eased before she replied. "I did. I have so much to tell you, but I have even more exciting news to share first." She held her hand out to him. "I want you to meet someone."

Stepping forward, he caught his first full glimpse of her mother. His heart clenched. She looked so diminutive amongst the cushions and blankets.

"Mum, this is Lucas."

"You should have warned me, hey." Her eyes widened as a fragile hand fluttered over her stringy hair. "I would have fixed myself up."

Lucas smiled. "You look more than presentable, Mrs. Anderson. I can see where Amelia gets her good looks from."

Vivian's hand lowered to press against her chest, and her lips quirked. "You could also have warned me he was a flatterer, Amelia."

Amelia laughed. "Well, today's a day for surprises—and it's time to reveal our main one." She met his gaze and nodded before sinking to her knees beside her mother and clasping her hands. "Lucas has something to ask you."

"Oh? And what's that?" Vivian angled her head and studied him as he pulled out one of the chairs from the nearby table and placed it in front of her.

He gulped. This wasn't as easy as he thought it would be. He felt like he was about to be interrogated. Maybe he was. He cleared his throat. "First, I want you to know you raised a very special young woman. But I'm sure you already know that."

She lifted a brow. "I don't think I can take much credit for that."

He shook his head. "You're her mother. You've played a vital role in Amelia's life whether you know it or not."

"Well, that's kind of you to say so, but she pretty much raised herself."

He glanced at Amelia, and they shared a knowing look. The poor woman. She truly was bereft of any worth. He was even more amazed by how Amelia had risen above her upbringing.

"Regardless, she loves you."

Her eyes misted. She sniffed. "You'd better get on to what you were going to say."

Swallowing hard, he leaned forward. "Mrs. Anderson, I've asked Amelia to marry me, and she said yes. But we'd love your blessing. It would mean the world to us." He reached out and squeezed Amelia's hand, her palm cool, clammy. He smiled his encouragement as he squeezed it again.

Her mother's gaze shifted between them. He was unsure if she was happy or otherwise until a smile broadened her thin face. "You don't need my blessing, but I'll gladly give it. This is exciting news. I hope I'll be around to see it happen."

A lump formed in his throat. Unless they acted swiftly, he doubted she would be.

"Thanks, Mum. That's wonderful." Amelia gave her a gentle hug while glancing at him, a sheen in her eyes, and his heart went out to them both.

They embraced for many moments before her mother waved to him. "I should give my future son-in-law a proper welcome. Come here."

Smiling, he edged closer and joined the hug. "Thank you, Mrs. Anderson. This means more to us than you know."

"No more of that Mrs. Anderson stuff. You're practically my son, aren't you? Mum will do just fine."

Amelia offered a watery smile.

He kissed the top of her head before smiling at her mother. "All right. Mum it is."

Chapter Eighteen

A lump formed in Amelia's throat as she gazed into the full-length mirror in Mike and Sheila's guest bedroom. Speechless, she let her gaze travel over her silky wedding gown as it cascaded to the floor in luxurious waves. A smooth, cream-coloured sash girded her waist, and the sweetheart neckline flattered her slight frame. The effect was simple yet elegant.

Staring at her reflection, she pinched herself. This was her wedding day! Marrying the man of her dreams with her mother there to witness it, surrounded by people who cared about her deeply, was a dream come true. The Lord had blessed her mightily, and she was so very grateful.

Willow adjusted the gorgeous diamond-encrusted hair clip given to Amelia by her mother-in-law-to-be and then stood back and beamed. "I always knew you'd be a beautiful bride, but you're even more exquisite than I could have imagined!"

She'd done a brilliant job on Amelia's makeup and hair, adding a touch of shimmer to her eyes and pulling her locks to the side and securing them with the clip. Simple, yet perfect.

Amelia smiled at her best friend. "All thanks to you. The dress is gorgeous. I love it."

Willow stepped closer and gripped Amelia's hands. "You're going to knock Lucas dead."

"I hope not." Amelia chuckled. "I want to marry him, not kill him."

Willow chuckled with her before sobering. "I'm so happy for you both, and I'm excited to be getting a sister, in both senses of the word."

Tipping her head, Amelia studied her sister-in-law-to-be. She and Willow *had* become like sisters over the months they'd known each other. Sisters in Christ, and now, they'd be sisters-in-law through marriage. How blessed she was. "Me too. I never thought I'd have a sister. Especially one like you."

"And what do you mean by that?"

"Nothing." She waved away Willow's mock crossness as Sheila appeared in the doorway.

"Okay for the mothers of the bride and groom to join you?"

Amelia beamed. "Of course. Come in."

The lump in her throat deepened as Sheila wheeled her mother into the room. How tiny she looked. She was slipping away, and yet a happiness radiated from her, a glow both contagious and beautiful.

Willow had piled what little hair Amelia's mother had left atop her head in a way that disguised its thinning state. The frothy lavender dress Willow created also somewhat hid her excruciating fragility, while silvery shoes matched the shellacked shimmer on her grey hair. A hint of blush, likely also Willow's touch, added a rosiness to her cheeks, but surely, the light radiating from her smile would have caused her face to shine without a single addition. Despite her mother's increasing frailty, Amelia had never seen her look so vibrant.

Her lips quivered as her gaze lifted to Amelia's. "I'd thought any hope of sharing this day with you was gone. But here we are."

Amelia leaned down and threaded her fingers through her mother's cold ones. "Yes, here we are. I'm so glad you're here, Mum." Bittersweet tears burned behind her eyes. Only God knew how much longer her mother had, but Amelia was committed to making every day, every moment, count.

Her mother reached up and adjusted one of the curls resting on Amelia's shoulder. "I'm very proud of you, Amelia. I know you're going to have a happy marriage."

She did her best to staunch her tears, but such emotion flowed through her some escaped and rolled down her cheek. "Thank you. That means so much."

"You're welcome." Her mother smiled. "Now, are you ready? It must be time. You don't want to keep your man waiting."

Amelia beamed. "I'm more than ready."

In a flash, Willow ushered her to the door and through the house. All three women gathered around her to help her into Sheila's car that they would take to the church. They'd return to the house later for the reception. Mike, Lucas, and Adam had done a fantastic job of transforming the garden into something special with string lights in the trees and a white tent beckoning in the breeze. Sheila and Willow had taken care of the flowers, adorning each table with a gorgeous centrepiece. They'd borrowed the Youth Centre's long crafting table to use for the potluck dishes and wedding cake.

If Charlotte had had her way, she'd have made the wedding a lavish affair that would have required months of planning. Sadly, Amelia's mum's condition made time a luxury they didn't have. After reuniting with her mother at last, Amelia couldn't imagine her not being a part of her big day. Lucas agreed and, utilizing the same efficiency with which he'd orchestrated the Youth Centre's opening, had made it possible for the wedding to take place a month after their engagement.

Her stomach fluttered as they drove towards the church.

Her mother reached over and gripped her hand. "You picked a very special young man. I know you two are going to be happy. And then once you start a family…"

Amelia's throat tightened. The fact that her mother would never meet her grandchildren came crashing down on her, though the reassurance the Lord quickly provided protected her heart. She squeezed her mother's hand. "I'm so grateful you're here to walk me down the aisle. It wouldn't be the same without you."

"No, it wouldn't." Sheila glanced at Amelia's mother. "And now you're living here in Water's Edge, you're fully expected to participate in the famous Kelley game night."

Her mum gave a weak chuckle. "That sounds like fun. Amelia can tell you how much I enjoy Scrabble."

"Game on!" Willow interjected from the front passenger seat.

"Careful. She might pull you into a match that'll last for weeks," Amelia teased. "Trust me, I've been there."

Her mother's eyes sparkled. "I can handle it. Consider it a challenge accepted."

With Charlotte's help, Amelia had managed to find a ground-floor apartment for her mother in Water's Edge. A full-time nurse had been employed, though Amelia visited daily.

The thought of her mum being unable to enjoy the new family she'd been taken into for long pained Amelia's heart. However, despite the hurt, no matter how much or how little time her mum had left on earth, every step of the journey was in God's hands. He'd proven His faithfulness thus far, giving her no reason not to trust Him further, even for her mother's salvation.

The church car park was full by the time they arrived.

"Get down, Amelia," Willow ordered.

"What?" Amelia laughed.

"Willow's right." Her mother gripped her hand. "We don't want anyone catching a peek of the bride before the big moment. Especially not the groom."

"I can just imagine him, standing at the altar, wondering what you'll look like." Willow's eyes twinkled, making Amelia's pulse quicken as she wondered what *he'd* look like.

Organ music drifted from the sanctuary when she alighted from the car with help from Willow and Sheila.

Willow adjusted her veil and train while Sheila helped Amelia's mum to her feet and handed her a walking stick. She was determined to walk down the aisle with Amelia, even though everyone had encouraged her to use the chair.

Hardly aware of the activity around her, Amelia closed her

eyes as the Lord's faithfulness and goodness overwhelmed her and her heart swelled with love for Him.

Thank You, Lord, for loving me enough to turn a life that was beating against You into one that could be used for Your glory. Take the life Lucas and I are about to start together into Your precious care. I entrust our union to You. Bless us and use us in whatever way You see fit.

"Are you ready, love?" Her mother smiled at her.

Nodding, Amelia looped her arm into her mother's.

Willow handed her a bouquet of white roses, taking up the smaller bunch she'd be carrying as maid of honour.

Not a single word was needed as Amelia and her mother followed Willow through the breezeway to the sanctuary doors.

The bridal march radiated from the organ as the double doors opened, revealing pews filled with well-wishers, friends, and family. Wonderful as the smiling faces were, Amelia only had eyes for the man at the end of the aisle—Lucas.

Her breath caught at the sight of his smiling face. He looked dashing in his tuxedo, but her heart would have beat the same if he were wearing jeans and a hoodie.

Thoughts of her redemption story flooded her as she and her mum began their steady walk towards the front platform.

Nothing had turned out the way she'd expected. It was better. When she'd arrived in Water's Edge, her only objective had been survival. Instead, God had surpassed her expectations, redeeming her more thoroughly than she'd ever believed possible. Being offered the blessing of taking the man before her as her husband was simply above and beyond. But that's what God did.

Lucas grasped her hand as her mother slipped into the front pew beside Sheila.

He beamed at her. "Are you ready?"

She reached up to caress his precious face. "Absolutely. I'm ready for anything and everything that comes next—as long as we're together and God's with us."

Epilogue

Four months later...

"All right, everyone, great job on constructing your arks. I have a feeling Noah himself would be proud." The kids gathered around the Youth Centre's craft table beamed under Lucas's praise as they eyed the miniature sea vessels they'd built with wood scraps from one of his recent construction jobs.

"The glue needs to dry if we want the arks to remain seaworthy, so what do you say we head out to the playground for recess before Bible study?"

Enthusiasm met his suggestion, and the kids were quick to rush to the door. His heart flipped when Amelia appeared before any of them had a chance to exit the recreation room. They'd been married for months, but the flutter his wife's mere presence caused within him had not subsided in the least.

The children bounced at the sight of her. She grinned as multiple kids spoke to her at once.

He stood back, smiling at the touching sight.

Once she was able to make it through the throng, she joined him near the craft table. "Well, hello, there."

"Wasn't sure you were going to make it through the crowd," he teased, slipping his arm around her waist.

"Sweet as they are, nothing would keep me from you. Not today."

His brows rose. "Only today?"

Laughing, she wrapped her arms around him. "Well, that applies to every day, but today is special because I have something I can't wait to tell you."

"Really?" His brows lifted further. "Go on."

Taking a deep breath, she pulled back and fished a letter from the back pocket of her jeans. She held it out to him.

"What's this?" he asked as he took it.

"Open it and find out."

He removed the letter from the envelope, his eyes widening as he read. "Nursing school? You've been accepted into nursing school in Sydney?"

She clasped her hands beneath her chin, nodding, excitement shining in her eyes. "Yes! I couldn't have done it without Dr. Turner's glowing recommendation. I'll have to commute, but I'm sure we can figure—"

He silenced her with a kiss. "Sweetheart, I'm so proud of you," he murmured when they broke apart.

She shook her head. "Just when I thought God had gifted me with everything I could ever want. I can hardly believe it."

"I can," he replied.

Her eyes misted. "I wish Mum could have been here. She'd be so happy."

He took her in his arms. "Yes, she would."

Vivian's final weeks in Water's Edge had consisted of bittersweet days that neither would forget. The restoration of Amelia and her mum's relationship was something to be treasured. However, Vivian's acceptance of Jesus as her Lord and Saviour only a week before she passed was the greatest gift of all.

"She'd be so proud of you," Lucas whispered against her hair. "But can I tell you something? She already was. And so am I."

Amelia chattered about the future as they left the recreation room. He listened in appreciative silence.

As they made their way through the Youth Centre that had once been only a dream for him and out into the sunshine where the children were playing, he marvelled at God's faithfulness in taking broken lives and turning them into something precious and beautiful. If that wasn't enough, He went on to bless those previously broken people beyond measure after making them whole.

Lucas surveyed the kids he was fortunate enough to mentor. Not a day would go by when he wouldn't communicate this reality to them with everything he had. Their God was One who restored His people and blessed them with every good thing.

Amelia was his greatest blessing. The day he met her his life irrevocably changed for the better. What a blessed man he was.

Because of the Lord's great love we are not consumed, for His compassions never fail. They are new every morning; great is Your faithfulness.

NOTE FROM THE AUTHOR

I hope you enjoyed "When I Met You" and were blessed by it. Amelia and Lucas's story continues in "Because of You" which will release in March 2022. I hope you're excited as I am to see how the story unfolds. You can pre-order your copy here and enjoy the first chapter below.

To ensure you don't miss any of my new releases, why not join my Readers' list http://www.julietteduncan.com/linkspage/282748 ? You'll also receive a free thank-you copy of "Hank and Sarah - A Love Story", a clean love story with God at the center.

Enjoyed "When I Met You"? You can make a big difference. Help other people find this book by writing a review and telling them why you liked it. Honest reviews of my books help bring them to the attention of other readers just like yourself, and I'd be very grateful if you could spare just five minutes to leave a review (it can be as short as you like) on the book's Amazon page.

Keep reading for your bonus chapter of "Because of You".

Blessings,
Juliette

Chapter 1 - Because of You

When the bell over the front door of The Coffee Bean Café jangled, Willow Kelley looked up. She smiled as Charlotte, owner of the local diner and a dear friend to just about everyone in the small town of Water's Edge, approached the counter.

"Good morning, Charlotte. Would you like your usual?"

"That would be wonderful, Willow. You know me so well."

Though anyone would have learned Charlotte's order after serving her every day for two years, Willow accepted the compliment. The older woman had been a little extra kind lately and she knew why. When you live in a small town, everyone knows the details of everyone else's life, so the fact that the past six months hadn't been easy for Willow was no secret.

It was nice to be looked out for, but the last thing she wanted was to be pitied for her misfortune. But she had to admit that if *she* were in the townspeople's shoes, she would have felt pity for her situation. Who wouldn't?

"How are things at the diner?" Willow asked as she pulled two espresso shots for Charlotte's flat white.

"Busy as usual," Charlotte replied, taking a bite of the apple crumb pastry Willow had already served her. "It's been difficult to find someone to replace Amelia. She's such a reliable girl and we sure miss having her. But things change and I'm so happy she's able to put time into school and help Lucas at the Youth Centre."

Though Willow was happy for her brother and sister-in-law, the reminder that some people got their happy ending pricked her heart as she frothed the milk for Charlotte's coffee. "Yes, she's definitely enjoying her nursing studies."

Charlotte's brow lowered. "And how are you enjoying *your* schooling? You two girls are carpooling to the city each week, aren't you?"

"Yes," Willow answered as she rang up Charlotte's order at the register. "It's going well. The college definitely has a good fashion design program." Her tone sounded lackadaisical even to her own ears. For years, it had been her dream to own her own boutique, and fashion design school was the first step in that pursuit.

Classes had started right after she met Jason and were everything she'd hoped they'd be, but her optimism about the future had seriously dimmed in all aspects since her divorce, even her design dreams.

The look on Charlotte's face made it clear that she was anything but convinced. The way her hair was piled up on her head creating a white halo and the softness around her wrinkled eyes made her look like a grandmotherly, guardian angel. "If it's so good, why don't you sound more excited?"

It was foolish to try and pretend. This kind woman could see right through her. "I guess I'm having trouble mustering the enthusiasm I once had."

Charlotte's face grew compassionate. "It's difficult to keep your excitement up in light of everything that's happened, isn't it?"

Willow gave a nod. Yep. She had that right.

"Trials like the one you've endured do quite a number on just about every aspect of a person's life."

She completely understood the sentiment behind Charlotte's words, but she couldn't think of anyone else who'd gone through what she had. Divorce after a year, yes. But after a month? She didn't personally know *anyone* whose marriage had dissolved that quickly. It made her feel all the more as if she'd done something wrong, that perhaps *she* was the problem since the other women around her had somehow managed to pick upstanding men.

What had she missed?

"It hasn't been easy," she admitted, placing Charlotte's change on the counter. "But life goes on, you know?"

Charlotte leaned in closer. "You're being very brave. I know that you have the support of your family, but if you ever need a shoulder to cry on, you know where to find me."

If only crying it out was all she needed. Her emotions regarding the situation were far more complex.

Would she ever heal from Jason's betrayal?

Would she ever be able to convince herself to move on, let alone love again?

CHAPTER 1 - BECAUSE OF YOU

Would she ever be able to trust God again?

She forced a smile. "Thanks, Charlotte. What do you have on the agenda for the day?" She was desperate to get the conversation off of her.

"The first order of business is to get the guest bedroom ship shape. My nephew's coming to stay for a few months. He just finished his electrician training in Sydney. Did Lucas mention they've hired Declan to do some work on the new recreation room at the Youth Centre?"

"I think Lucas did mention something about it," Willow replied half-heartedly. "That's very nice."

"It'll be nice to have company," Charlotte remarked. "I'll introduce you two as soon as possible."

"Sounds good." But honestly, Willow cared little about meeting new people. All she wanted was for things to go back to the way they were before her heart was broken.

Back when she was happy.

Back when she trusted God.

Grab your copy here: http://www.julietteduncan.com/linkspage/2216471

Other Books by Juliette Duncan

Find all of Juliette Duncan's books on her website: www.julietteduncan.com/library

Water's Edge Series

When I Met You

A barmaid searching for purpose, a youth pastor searching for love

Because of You

When dreams are shattered, can hope be re-found?

A Sunburned Land Series

A mature-age romance series

Slow Road to Love

A divorced reporter on a remote assignment. An alluring cattleman who captures her heart...

Slow Path to Peace

With their lives stripped bare, can Serena and David find peace?

Slow Ride Home

He's a cowboy who lives his life with abandon. She's spirited and fiercely independent...

Slow Dance at Dusk

A death, a wedding, and a change of plans...

Slow Trek to Triumph

A road trip, a new romance, and a new start...

The Shadows Series

A jilted teacher, a charming Irishman, & the chance to escape their pasts & start again.

Lingering Shadows

Facing the Shadows

Beyond the Shadows

Secrets and Sacrifice

A Highland Christmas

True Love Series

Tender Love

Tested Love

Tormented Love

Triumphant Love

Precious Love Series

Forever Cherished

Forever Faithful

Forever His

A Time For Everything Series

A mature-age Christian Romance series

A Time to Treasure

She lost her husband and misses him dearly. He lost his wife but is ready to move on. Will a chance meeting in a foreign city change their lives forever?

A Time to Care

They've tied the knot, but will their love last the distance?

A Time to Abide

When grief hovers like a cloud, will the sun ever shine again for Wendy?

A Time to Rejoice

He's never forgiven himself for the accident that killed his mother. Can he find forgiveness and true love?

Transformed by Love Christian Romance Series

Because We Loved

Because We Forgave

Because We Dreamed

Because We Believed

Because We Cared

Billionaires with Heart Series

Her Kind-Hearted Billionaire

A reluctant billionaire, a grieving young woman, and the trip *that changes their lives forever...*

Her Generous Billionaire

A grieving billionaire, a devoted solo mother, and a woman determined to sabotage their relationship...

Her Disgraced Billionaire

A billionaire in jail, a nurse who cares, and the challenge that changes their lives forever...

Her Compassionate Billionaire

A widowed billionaire with three young children. A replacement nanny who helps change his life...

The Potter's House Books...

Stories of hope, redemption, and second chances. *The Homecoming*

Can she surrender a life of fame and fortune to find true love?

Blessings of Love

She's going on mission to help others. He's going to win her heart.

The Hope We Share

Can the Master Potter work in Rachel and Andrew's hearts and give them a second chance at love?

The Love Abounds

Can the Master Potter work in Megan's heart and save her marriage?

Love's Healing Touch

A doctor in need of healing. A nurse in need of love.

Melody of Love

She's fleeing an abusive relationship, he's grieving his wife's death...

Whispers of Hope

He's struggling to accept his new normal. She's losing her patience...

Heroes Of Eastbrooke Christian Suspense Series

Safe in His Arms

SOME SAY HE'S HIDING. HE SAYS HE'S SURVIVING

Under His Watch

HE'LL STOP AT NOTHING TO PROTECT THOSE HE LOVES. NOTHING.

Within His Sight

SHE'LL STOP AT NOTHING TO GET A STORY. HE'LL SCALE THE HIGHEST MOUNTAIN TO RESCUE HER.

Freed by His Love

HE'S DRIVEN AND DETERMINED. SHE'S BROKEN AND SCARED.

Stand Alone Christian Romantic Suspense

Leave Before He Kills You

When his face grew angry, I knew he could murder...

The Madeleine Richards Series

Although the 3 book series is intended mainly for pre-teen/Middle Grade girls, it's been read and enjoyed by people of all ages. Here's what one reader had to say about it: *"Juliette has a fabulous way of bringing her characters to life. Maddy is at typical teenager with authentic views and actions that truly make it feel like you are feeling her pain and angst. You want to enter into her situation and make everything better. Mom and soon to be dad respond to her with love and gentle persuasion while maintaining their faith and trust in Jesus, whom they know, will give them wisdom as they continue on their lives journey. Appropriate for teenage readers but any age can enjoy."* Reader

About the Author

Juliette Duncan is a USA Today bestselling author of Christian romance stories that 'touch the heart and soul'. She lives in Brisbane, Australia and writes Christian fiction that encourages a deeper faith in a world that seems to have lost its way. Most of her stories include an element of romance, because who doesn't love a good love story? But the main love story in each of her books is always God's amazing, unconditional love for His wayward children.

Juliette and her husband enjoy spending time with their five adult children, eight grandchildren, and their elderly, long-haired dachshund, Chipolata (Chip for short). When not writing, Juliette and her husband love exploring the wonderful world they live in.

Connect with Juliette:

Email: author@julietteduncan.com

Website: www.julietteduncan.com

Facebook: www.facebook.com/JulietteDuncanAuthor

Made in United States
Troutdale, OR
07/06/2024